About the Author

Amber Deckers grew up in South Africa where she studied film, before going on to work for an advertising agency. During this time, she was a part-time journalism student and eventually joined *Marie Claire* as a features and fashion writer and book reviewer.

Deciding to swap the shores of Africa for London, Amber worked for various publishers in London before joining an independent film production company with the idea of creating a television programme about teenage issues. When the project was shelved, Amber decided to put her research and ideas into a novel, which became *Ella Mental and the Good Sense Guide*, published by Orchard in 2005. The sequel, *Ella Mental – Life, Love and More Good Sense*, followed in 2006.

Amber and her husband Craig live in Surrey with their sons Tay and Brodie. Amber currently works as a freelance journalist whilst also working on her next book.

For Brodie Archie Aitken,
who made our world complete

ORCHARD BOOKS
338 Euston Road, London NW1 3BH

Orchard Books Australia
Level 17/207 Kent Street, Sydney, NSW 2000

A paperback original

First published in Great Britain in 2008
Text copyright © Amber Deckers 2008

The right of Amber Deckers to be identified as the author of this work
has been asserted by her in accordance with the Copyright, Designs and
Patents Act, 1988.

A CIP catalogue record for this book is available from the British Library

ISBN 978 1 84616 302 9

1 3 5 7 9 10 8 6 4 2

Typeset by SX Composing DTP, Rayleigh, Essex
Printed in Great Britain

Orchard Books is a division of Hachette Children's Books,
an Hachette Livre UK company.

www.hachettelivre.co.uk

The Pursuit of Liberty Belle

Amber Deckers

ORCHARD BOOKS

Part One
Before

one
and they call this fun?

Divorce can have a silver lining. Take birthdays and Christmas, for example: you're supposed to get double the gifts and double the treats. Or so I've heard. My friend Kate is on her second divorce (on her mum's side) and she's Little Miss Got-It-All. She's always well stocked with all the coolest clothes and latest CDs and has a bedroom jamming with super-fancy gadgets. And ever since her father proposed to his girlfriend she seems to spend every holiday in a place that's warm and sandy. Some divorcees don't have it half bad – they have it doubly good.

Daisy, who sits next to me in Biology, has it different. Her mum was a teenage mum – just like mine, but her parents were married for twelve months, not years. Her father disappeared immediately A.D. (After Divorce) and she can't even remember her parents being together, so perhaps she doesn't really count as divorced. I mean, what can she honestly know about it? She's only met the man her mother calls Mr-Two-Minutes-Behind-the-Bike-Shed once since then and she didn't like him one bit. She doesn't get on much better with her mum, mind you. Daisy's mum has had more boyfriends than Mr-Two-Minutes-Behind-the-Bike-Shed has tattoos. They say you can choose your friends but you can't choose your family. Whoever *they* are, they may have a point.

My own divorce was nothing like Kate's or Daisy's. My parents met when they were both students at college, although they weren't ever really girlfriend and boyfriend. Like Daisy, I was what you might call 'an accident' (although I don't believe there was ever a bike shed involved). My mum says that many of the world's greatest wonders are accidental – a chance grain of trapped sand transformed into a glistening pearl, is her favourite example. Speaking of miracles, I think it's a miracle my mother and father even found themselves in the same room. They have zip in common. My father is a head man; my mum is all heart. My father thinks control, discipline and regular gym workouts will make this world a better place; my mum is a hippy New Age nature freak who will gladly hug a tree, a complete stranger or her best friend – they're all the same to her. My father has a responsible nine-to-fiver that pays him enough money to live comfortably and save a bit every month; my mum teaches yoga and meditation classes – sometimes for free – drives a dinosaur car and will survive, quite happily, on organic beans on toast if she has to.

My parents divorced less than two years ago but my father's already married his personal fitness trainer, Misty the ex-Mistress. They even have a brand new baby called Thomas. My mum, on the other hand, has just started dating a bloke called Mick who wears cut-off denims and cowboy hats, even though he's not (a cowboy, that is). Not even close. It's no secret that my parents were counting the seconds until I turned twelve, which is precisely the day until they agreed to remain married (giving me a stable childhood, blah blah). Yes, a divorce was just what I needed to brighten up adolescence. It's no wonder I talk to myself like this. They say only crazy people talk to themselves, but I wonder if talking thoughts count as the same thing? That's what I call the voices – my talking thoughts. Yup, there's pretty much always a voice in my head making a comment about something and everything. And there's usually very little I can do to shut me up.

'Libby, it's your turn next.'

That was my father's voice, and it's my turn to bowl. I spent the last year convinced that I was going to die; now I'm just hoping I do. Maybe the fungal infection I'll almost certainly catch from these rental toe-jam tenpin bowling shoes will spread through my body and do me in, although that sounds like a slow death and hardly likely to save me from the agony of today. Typical. Nothing goes my way.

'I'm coming.' I sigh and heave-ho myself off the padded bench near the ball rack. I take my time in choosing one of the smaller hard black balls that still weighs as much as Stonehenge and ram my innocent fingers into the triangle of dark and dingy germ holes designed to grip the ball. I'm not a hygiene freak, but just imagining all the grubby stranger-fingers that have been here before me turns me green. With my luck all the nose pickers and bottom scratchers of the world will have chosen this very same ball. My life's like that.

I'm trying very hard not to look to my left at the group of kids who are about my age and occupying the lane two down from us. They're very loud and more interested in fooling about than bowling. They can't even speak the words *ball rack* without hooting, which of course has my father tut-tutting and shaking his head in disapproval. Gripping the infested ball, I estimate two steps from the line, which, according to tenpin bowling rules, I'm not allowed to cross over. And then I glance left. I just can't help it.

That same boy from ten minutes ago has suddenly made an appearance and is now standing exactly where I'm standing – only two lanes down from me, just like the last time it was my turn to bowl in the gutter. I look over – his eyes are laughing and mocking me. I notice a few other things about him too, like his dimpled chin and the bleached blond skunk stripe running through his dark hair, which is stand-up straight with gel.

I give him my well-rehearsed *oh-please-I'm-so-bored* grimace (drives the father insane) and turn my attention back to the pale wooden alley before me. Now all I have to do is hit those stupid white pins that look like milk bottles at the end of the lane with this seven-pound booger ball. It can't be that difficult, I keep reminding myself. My lack of self-belief is what usually limits me more than my actual ability to do most things. I'm just about to begin my run-up when Skunk Boy two lanes down begins coughing and spluttering and loudly demanding silence so that he can concentrate on his bowling. I pause with my ball midair, flip my eyes diva-style and immediately launch my ball into the air (I really just want to get this over with). With my fingers safely returned to me I would usually turn right around and simply walk away, leaving the ball to fall where it may. Like, *who cares*? But today I'm mesmerised by the sweeping arc it's cutting through the air. It almost seems to be soaring in slow motion, like something wild and beautiful and weightless that's finally been set free. The ball revolves as it flies and every now and again I catch a brief glimpse of the triangle of black shapes I know are holes. Liberated from filthy fingers and rigid racks and dirty gutters, my bowling ball is finally flying and spinning and twirling through the air like a breathtaking circus act released from its cage.

And then suddenly it drops like a meteorite, crashing into the pale wooden strips of the lane with a splintering and resounding thwack! But it hasn't even landed in the right lane. My liberated bowling ball is now crawling wounded down the lane next door, which is also the lane that runs alongside Skunk Boy and his wild forest friends, who are actually silent and spellbound for the first time today. Even my talking thoughts have muted. They say it's always quiet before the storm.

Like a chorus cued by a patient conductor, my peers suddenly start cackling and hooting, shouting out things like 'Ball buster!' Sometimes I don't know my own strength. I obviously don't know how to aim either.

All of a sudden a voice bounces off the alley walls. It's loud and booming and bold enough to beat all the other voices into submission.

'Would you all please quieten down and return to your own games!' I knew God would come to my rescue if I prayed hard enough. 'This is by order of the Management.' Perhaps God is working through the Management. Either way, calm seems to have been restored.

Skunk Boy is still clutching his own bowling ball and, with a wink, he takes a determined stride forward and half kneels in the get-set position before effortlessly releasing his grip on the bowling ball. I don't even have to look. The crash-bang explosion of bowling-ball-annihilating pins is unmistakable. So are Skunk Boy's whoops.

My father is muttering and waiting for me in our booth. 'There's no point in attracting the attention of youngsters like that, Liberty,' he reprimands me as I slump back into the padded bench near the ball rack. Ball rack, ha ha. 'And as for your last bowling attempt…'

'I didn't do that on purpose!' I bite back.

'Don't you take that tone with me, young lady. All I'm saying is that you really could have tried a bit harder.'

That's my father's attitude towards everything: there's always room for improvement. That's because nothing is ever good enough for him. I've heard him telling Misty that if he keeps raising the bar I'll keep reaching higher. Misty replied that she thought I was legally too young to drink.

She wasn't trying to be funny – she's just not the smartest person in the world. There are two more things I know with conviction about my father's new wife. The first is that she still knows absolutely nothing about me. And that includes my age, what school I attend, what year I'm in, what food I like or what my interests are. She's got my first name memorised and that's about it, although I have caught her looking at me strangely before, as if trying to place me. I don't take offence; Misty doesn't do it to be mean. She's just too busy thinking about other things. That's another thing I know about Misty: she's obsessed with her looks and likes to focus on her body's muscle-to-fat ratio. She's already made the cover of two fitness magazines and her dream is to make her own workout video. That's two more things I know about my father's new wife.

'I'll hold Thomas, it's your turn to bowl,' my father orders Misty, who has been rocking my baby half-brother in her arms and admiring the swell of her toned biceps at the same time.

'Oh, I don't think so, Mackenzie,' she whimpers. 'I've

just had my nails done.' And she's right. She has. They're long and plastic and painted sherbet pink – Misty's favourite colour. 'I think I'll just sit here and watch Thomas.' If only her beautiful biceps weren't so distracting.

'Sometimes I just don't know why I bother,' my father grumbles out loud. 'Righty-ho then, I'll bowl next and then you can have another go at it, Liberty.'

'No thanks, I have officially retired from bowling.' My dignity and I are staying put.

'We might as well have stayed at home!' he snaps. Finally we're on the same page, the talking thoughts cheer. 'This was meant to be a special day for you, Liberty. You're spending the next three weeks at Your Mother's and yet all you have for your family is a couldn't-care-less attitude.'

'This is meant to be *my* birthday,' I remind him. 'And I didn't even want to go bowling – you did!' My birthday is actually in two days' time but it falls during the school holidays, which means I'll be with my mum in Brighton. I spend every holiday and some weekends in Brighton, which is not nearly as many as I'd like. But at least this year I'm spending Christmas with my mum too.

Beyond my father Skunk Boy's group are raucous and

just the vent my father needs. He executes a sudden 180-degree turn on the rubber heel of his size ten blue-and-red-striped bowling shoe and marches over to the noise with his elbows swinging from side to side like a wind-up toy. He comes to a standstill with his nose only inches from Skunk Boy, who looks surprised but not concerned.

'Young man,' Mackenzie Belle huffs, 'you and your friends have ruined what should have been a decent day out for me and my family. You have been loud and disruptive and made it practically impossible for my daughter Liberty to bowl a decent ball.'

Oh, please nooo! The mention of my name pushes me lower, pressing me into the seat's depths. My skin and the red fake-leather backrest have almost melted into one. My father dreams of perfection – of the ideal, well-ordered little family. And if he can find someone else to blame for today's disaster then that'll mean he can continue with the delusion that he's the head of a smiley, fully-functioning family unit for just a little while longer. Then we just might still stand a chance of being the perfect family.

Skunk Boy grins cheekily. 'Me and my mates have been minding our own business. It's your daughter who made a scene by throwing her ball into the lane next to ours. We can't help it if we found that funny now, can we? Funny is funny.'

The fever that ignited my cheeks has now spread like wildfire across my entire body, burning me up from the inside out. I really *have* melted into the red fake-leather seat cushion.

'Would you like it if other people laughed at you?' my father counters. *Oh no, he thinks he's coming to my defence!*

'My mates laugh at me all the time.' Skunk Boy is grinning comically.

'Well, this is entirely different. My daughter was trying her best to tenpin bowl. Your fool-about antics weren't making it any easier for her.'

'It's a free world, mister.' Skunk Boy laughs as he leans past my father's steaming head. Now he's looking directly at me. 'But I'd be happy to give Liberty a few bowling lessons, if she's up for it. I think she may have some potential.' He raises his eyebrows at me. I'm so embarrassed I think I'm going to be sick.

'Unlike you!' my father snorts furiously. 'If you don't change your attitude you'll never amount to anything.' This is my father's parting shot; he about-turns and marches, elbows swinging, back over to our booth. 'Come on, we're leaving!' he barks and starts gathering up Thomas's various baby paraphernalia. Misty looks confused but no more than usual and quickly returns Thomas to his buggy. This is all too much for me and I'm about to make a rapid exit when I spy my father standing with a baby bottle in one hand, a stuffed Tweenie toy in the other and an overstuffed baby-blue nappy bag over his shoulder, scowling at Skunk Boy and his posse. He thinks he looks menacing. If only the walls were mirrored. Maybe I should just try laughing at my problems – everyone else does.

Email is the umbilical cord to my other life in Brighton. It's not easy having two lives but modern technology definitely helps. I receive emails from Mum at least once a week and Sam, my closest friend in the entire world, sends me an email every single day. Sometimes two or three times a day. We also use Chat, which is like having a typed conversation.

When my father and Misty and Thomas have all gone to bed and the house in Manchester finally falls silent, Sam and I often stay up for hours furtively chatting in cyberspace – me sitting in my bedroom and Sam in Brighton, not too far from my mum and the ocean. Lucky Sam. And this is how, on a Friday in October at precisely 11.04 pm, Sam came to tell me that he loved me. I remember the exact moment – me staring at the screen for ever, watching the little cursor blinking rapidly in time with my heartbeat.

'You do know that I love you, Liberty Belle,' the screen said. Sam said. I read each one of his words a dozen times. The cursor was blinking so fast I thought it might explode.

'I love you too, Samir Pejic,' I finally replied with fingers trembling like Edmund Hillary at the summit of Mount Everest. And then I climbed inside my bed and had a small, emotional sob. I love Sam. And I miss him. Just like I love and miss my mum in Brighton. If I designed worlds I'd make sure that they were no bigger than where your legs could take you.

*

Sam, r u there?

Blink. Blink. Blink. Today the cursor seems slow and weak. Once or twice I think it may even have died on me. I'm just about to abandon my attempt and close Chat down when suddenly the cursor flickers back to life.

Sorry Libby, I got caught up helping Gloria with something. Mums, eh? Sigh! How r u?

Now that I have Sam at my fingertips I am fresh and new. The tenpin tragedy is gone and forgotten and I am mended.

I'm fine, Sam. Only 1 more sleep to go!!!

Yup, u missing me?

Could be. ☺

Blink. Blink. I glance up at the small mirror with its frame of driftwood that Sam made especially for me. I'm smiling right up to my eyes.

Well, I've missed you, Liberty Belle. Everything seems different when you're not around.

I think I know what he means. I seem to lose a part of me when I leave Brighton. Or maybe I just leave that part of me behind. I suspect that this may be my heart. I return to the keyboard and type:

We have almost 3 weeks this time. Our first Christmas 2!

Yeah, hope you've bought me something special. ;-)

Actually, I haven't bought him a bean yet. I've been looking in all the shop windows but so far I haven't seen the perfect gift. I'm hoping to find it in Brighton.

U will have to wait & c. How's my mum?

She's fine. Looking 4ward 2 cing u. We're coming to yr house 4 lunch on Saturday. Lotus was going 2 cook but Mick thankfully stepped in. Lotus was going 2 make artichoke soup. :-/

Mum and Lotus have been sharing a house for almost two years now so I'm used to their rather interesting New Age vegetarian dishes. Mum and Mick haven't been dating for nearly as long and my chest still tightens when I hear his name. Of course we like Mick, the thoughts hum repeatedly. I can't continue fighting the reality that my mother now has a boyfriend. So she's promised that no one could ever take my place and I'd like to believe her, but I can't seem to get past the fact that Mick gets to try 24/7, twelve months of the year. It's much easier to become someone's favourite when you put the time in.

My life is nothing if not ironic: the very things I love about my mum are the exact same reasons why it's been decided that I have to live with my father during school term. My mum doesn't subscribe to bureaucracy, global corporations, the power of the media or modern technology, banks, war, politics or social convention.

My nine-to-five father, meanwhile, has a three-bed semi in suburbia, a station wagon with dual airbags and a bank manager called Phil. He's everything society says I need in a parent and that's why I live in Manchester.

Hey, u still there, Libby?

I've been staring at the blinking cursor, tangled up in my thoughts long enough to defocus my eyes and turn the screen blurry. I shake my head to clear the water and centre my pupils.

Course. Bowling with the father and Misty was a DIS-AS-TER, btw.

I don't delve into the details though...or mention Skunk Boy – he's not worth it. And Sam might just get the wrong idea.

Don't worry – we have something special planned 4 yr birthday, Lib.

No fanfare pls!

2 late. And it's not up 2 u anywayz.

I think it's seriously vain 2 celebrate the day u were born.

I'd better take yr pressie back 2 the shop then.

I'm trying to think of something slick to say when suddenly the night-time quiet dead-ends in a scream that's loud, high-pitched and hungry. It's Thomas and he wants feeding. Again. I only have about forty seconds to end this Chat.

So sorry Sam, have 2 go.

Thomas just woke the house up, huh?

Sam knows my life's routines; that's what you do when you care. The thought warms me.

U know it. Speak 2morrow?

Course.

xx

xx

I quickly shut down the computer and watch the life being suddenly sucked out of the multi-coloured screen, leaving it dead and grey and lifeless. I know how it feels; my nights are pale and empty without Sam to talk to. My bedroom, once illuminated by the screen's glow, is now a contoured landscape of three-dimensional shadows with sharp edges and soft bulges. I know every corner and cove and quietly make my way over to the bed and slip stealthily beneath the still-cool covers.

Somewhere beyond my room somebody's opened a door. Now they're walking across the landing, heading in the direction of the nursery. It used to be that Misty would do the night-time feeds (boobage attached), but now that Tommy has switched to bottle feeding my reluctant father has been forcibly recruited into the midnight madness. And he's not silent about it either. The footsteps in the hallway are dragging heels first – a sure sign that it's his shift.

It'll take me a while to fall asleep but I've got the thoughts to keep me occupied. On a personal level, this bottle feeding business has its advantages and disadvantages. One advantage is that I don't have to suffer unexpected giant eyefuls of Misty's boobage any more. Feeding a baby on demand means that it can happen at any time, and any place. I've rounded too many corners too often and run straight into Misty. With her boobage out. Again. The fact that there was a baby attached didn't make it any easier (I mean, I hardly know the woman). Of course the downside to the bottle arrangement is my father's involvement. Once he's done feeding Tommy he likes to check on me. He's very nosy like that. I tried to explain to him that privacy is like oxygen to a teenager but he simply sighed, rolled his eyeballs to the back of his head and said something about rules and his roof. But that's typical of my father; Mum would never be that dismissive. She's always there to listen and willing to talk things through. Still, only one more sleep and then I have my holiday with her. And Sam. And the ocean.

three
it's to the sea for me

'Do hurry up, Liberty. We must leave in precisely fifteen minutes.'

That's my father's voice doling out instructions, as usual. But for once I don't mind his nagging. We have *precisely fifteen minutes* to get to the train station – to the train that will carry me all the way to Brighton. Choo choo, my talking thoughts toot merrily. It's been almost six weeks since my last visit and I feel cheerfully alive, like a small hopeful child. Woo hoo! There's just no stopping the thoughts today.

My clothes are folded and laid out on my bed in teetering piles, ready to be slipped inside my backpack. I really won't be taking all that much; I have some clothes at Mum's and besides, we always go shopping. It's a mother-daughter bonding ritual and a very necessary one at that. What my father knows about fashion is troubling and as for Misty – well, neon bum-hugging nylon is not my thing. Not that she's ever taken me shopping. She hasn't offered and I haven't asked. And I'd say we're both quite satisfied with this arrangement. What would we talk about? She's into nails you stick on, suntans you spray on and repetitive exercise. And I'm into…well, I'm not entirely sure what I'm into but it's none of the above. So we really have nothing in common. I begin wedging the tower of clothing into my backpack bit by bit before closing it up with a flourish. There's nothing better than that holiday feeling!

'Li-ber-ty!'

'Co-ming!'

Suddenly there's the sound of a car engine gunning in the driveway. I grab my backpack and scoot out into the hallway, pulling my bedroom door closed behind me – even though I know my father will open it again. We operate under an Open Door Policy. It's for my own good.

The drive to the station is short and uneventful and it's only when we're on the train platform that my father, who has Thomas curled inside his right arm, suddenly has something to say.

'OK, my girl, this is it then.'

He looks awkwardly nervous. And he hasn't called me 'my girl' since I was very young…definitely Before Divorce.

'Have a good time with Your Mother and don't worry about us.'

'Sure.' I nod, even though I wasn't anticipating any sleepless nights.

'And I'll call you later to make sure that you've arrived safely.'

'Sure.' (This time without the nod.)

'Call me if you need, uh, something.'

Nod. (We've had our full quotient of lectures thanks, the talking thoughts note.)

We stand there for a few moments, our jackets dancing in the winter wind while we rock on our heels and glance at each other self-consciously. It's my father who makes the first move and with one stride forward places his free hand on my shoulder and kisses each one of my cheeks with his outstretched lips. They feel warm and dry on my skin. I can also smell his aftershave. The sweet clean smell makes my uptight father – the very same man who has his house rules laminated – suddenly seem a bit more human. And I realise, rather surprisingly, that he probably can't help himself or change the fact that he's a freak for rules and discipline. He's just not one of life's smiley-bendy people; he simply wasn't built that way. Maybe it's not really his fault.

So I put a hand over his and settle my left cheek against his left cheek. I don't stay there long, mind you – just long enough to transform right now into a heartfelt moment for two. To curious commuters the gesture might look like a dry hug, but for us this is definitely warm and fuzzy.

'Right then,' we say out loud and in unison and take one step backwards. The air gushing in to fill the new space between us is fresh and cold.

'Give Your Mother my best,' he adds politely. I know the only thing he'd really like to give my mother is a maintenance summons (he thinks a 'proper job' will do her the world of good), but right now he's trying his best to do what he thinks is proper and right.

The air is silent while I attempt to think of something to say. I know precisely what he wants me to say. His solemn face reads: 'Now it's your turn.' He wants me to leave him with a heartfelt message for Misty, who was at the gym attending a body-sculpting class when we left for the train station.

'Bye Thomas,' I finally say and then kiss his soft chubby cheek. More silence. My chin is raised ever so slightly in defiance; the muscle in my father's left jawbone is pulsing like he's eaten something alive. Warm and fuzzy just went the way of summer.

At that moment the platform conductor, dressed in stiff blue with a matching cap, blows his whistle – twice, hard and sharp.

'And tell Misty I said bye.' Of course I'd rather not give in, but right now it's the quickest and easiest way to conclude this moment. And at least I never said *good* bye. That's my silent little victory.

'Yes, I'll do that.' He nods and attempts a small, hard smile.

I give my father and Thomas a short wave and immediately head for the closest train door without looking back once. I know he'll do the same – turn around and head for the exit. We've had our sentimental moment.

It's been a busy morning and as the train lurches and begins slowly chugging forward, I feel my limbs loosening and my eyelids descending. I really thought that today excitement would beat fatigue hands down, but the world in all its colour is being squeezed out of sight by the spreading blackness. And there's not a thing I can do to stop it.

I must have been really tired, because I end up sleeping almost all the way to Brighton and only wake up again when something collides with my forehead. It hurts too. The pain jolts me wide awake and I stare around me in wonder. There's drool on my chin. I'm still on the train, which is slowing and beginning its stop-start crawl into our destination station.

The sharp pain across my forehead appears to be courtesy of the old lady who was sitting across from me but is now standing and swaying dangerously with a roll of boiled sweets clutched inside one veined hand. The other hand is clutching a walking stick – a cane one, the very kind that would cause some pain, should it come crashing into someone's sleeping skull. There's a reason why you're supposed to remain seated until the train comes to a full stop. I glare pointed eyeballs at the old lady but she's oblivious to my efforts and sucking noisily on a sweet while humming an upbeat tune only someone born in black and white might recognise. So I stare out of the window instead and watch people rushing and electronic signboards streaming with information and pigeons blinking at the busyness – too daft to fly off to a place far prettier and more peaceful than this station. If I were a bird I'd live in a palm tree in the Bahamas for sure.

Mum and Sam are waiting for me on the train station platform. Mick – my mum's boyfriend – is standing beside them. I've been waiting for this moment for so long, and why Chicken Mick had to come along too is beyond rational thought. So he's not the worst guy in the world, but this isn't his special moment. Must he take everything from me?

And it seems that not even winter's pinnacle is enough to tempt him into covering up his legs. He's still wearing those same cut-off denim shorts with their ridiculous trailing tattered hems. Someone should tell the man that the Sixties died. And his legs definitely still look like chicken drumsticks. The thoughts are evidently feeling mean today. I wade through the pigeons and passengers with bags, dipping my left eye down to half mast so as to reduce Mick to a watery blur. Now all I have to do is decide who to go to first – Mum or Sam. It's not easy loving and missing two people so much.

Mum hasn't changed one bit. Her hair is still

boy-short and as white as a goose. She's dressed in her favourite white muslin top and flowing embroidered trousers that reveal the tops of her shoes, which are made out of fabric printed with jade and cerise flowers. I suppose someone should break the news of the death of the Sixties to Mum too, but somehow she manages to look super-hippie-lovely and I can't resist tipping headfirst into her open arms dangling with colourful handmade jewellery. As she sucks me against her warmth and wraps me up inside her circle of beads and bracelets it hits me that I'm finally home. And home has nothing to do with Brighton. Her smell, the feel of her…nothing has changed. Here I am safe, here I am loved. This is where I began; she was all I knew when my world was dark and watery. Back then it was just the two of us. I listen for her familiar heartbeat. The sound of her drumming is unforgettable.

'I've missed you so much,' I gush hoarsely into her muslin.

When she finally prises me away and gently lifts my chin up to her face she's smiling through eyes that are like pale glass blurred by the rain. 'I've missed you too, Libby.'

A busker with a guitar suddenly starts singing and *bam!* I'm back on the station platform, fully conscious of everyone around us. Sam is still waiting for me; he's also just as lovely as ever. His wavy hair is still thick and black and his smile is still a glimmer with white teeth just skew enough to be interesting. And those eyes...one dark and one a pale blue colour. They're unforgettable, just like Sam. I rush into his arms. Ah, the smell of Christmas spice – I hadn't forgotten. But not everything is the same. He feels slightly thicker and stronger this time around, like a pumped-up version of his old skinny self.

'Have you been working out?' I laugh into his curls.

'Oh no,' he replies, releasing me and waving his hands with an air of debonair dismissal. 'I am naturally blessed with this spectacular physique.' His pursed lips are the only thing keeping his laughter locked up tight.

'Oh please, he's been lifting weights seven days a week!' This new voice is deep and chuckling good-humouredly. Ah yes, Chicken Mick – I had hoped to ignore him for a little while longer. But I can't block him out for ever so I slowly turn to face the man who stole my mum's heart.

'Hiya Mick.' I say that mostly for my mother and because it's good manners. But I won't move to hug him.

'Hello there, Liberty.' He continues grinning his big smiley grin. I really wish he wouldn't, but maybe being nice is part of his big plan to overthrow my world. 'So how was your trip?' asks Chicken Mick, now a.k.a. Captain of the Coup. He's still grinning. Yes, he's definitely good at this.

'Well, there was a train. And I sat inside it. For about five hours,' I conclude with a sweet smile. Mum's eyebrows instantly narrow to a V. Already I'm pushing the boundaries. 'So, uh, it was fine. Thanks.' I try to make this last bit sound more sincere.

'Glad to hear it,' Mum says, ruffling my hair tenderly. 'Shall we get going? Mick's car is parked around the corner.'

Of course it is. Pity, I've almost missed Aurora – Mum's battered old purple Alfa Romeo. 'Sure.' I beam stiffly. Mick quickly falls in step with Mum and takes her hand while Sam sidles up closer to me and takes my bag.

'I can manage that,' I huff without even really meaning to.

Sam scrunches up his face and growls at me playfully. 'Grrrr.'

'OK…OK.' I shrug and grin, surrendering the bag. Sam is always telling me to chill out. He's the only one who can make my hard edges soft. And besides, I've been waiting for this day and this moment for so long it seems silly to throw it away simply because Mick is here. I mean, apart from the ridiculous denim-shorts-à-la-hot-pants he insists on wearing come blizzard or shine he's really not such a bad bloke. I mean, if my mum insists on having a boyfriend then I suppose he's not the worst there is. Some of my divorced mates at school have some strange parent boyfriends and girlfriends to contend with. The thoughts can be optimistic; they're not all bad. Sam is staring at me.

'Whaaat?'

'Nothing. I just missed you heaps, that's all.' He smiles and rolls his shoulders sheepishly.

'I missed you too,' I utter just loud enough for the words to fall short of Mum's and Mick's ears.

'So how are things at home?'

'I *am* home,' I reply quickly, simply because it makes me feel better.

'I mean with your fa—'

'I know what you mean,' I interrupt him with a sigh. 'Manchester is fine. Brigadier General Mackenzie Belle is fine. Misty the Workout Barbie is fine. And little Thomas is really cute and sweet. He squawks a lot but it keeps the other two busy so I'm not complaining.'

Sam chuckles but doesn't add anything further. He knows all about my dull life in Manchester and he has the good sense not to add any commentary. Some things you can't change or improve on.

'So how's Gloria then?'

'She's waiting for us at your mum's, and she's the same as always.' Sam grins, obviously thinking a happy thought about his unconventional mother. 'Only this time she's taken up fire walking.'

'Never!'

'Yup. She's walking barefoot across hot coals for fun.'

'But why?' I'm trying not to laugh.

'She's uh…testing her beliefs about the nature of reality – or that's what she keeps telling me anyway. She calls it an unforgettable example of human potential. She'd be very entertaining at a barbeque, I'll give her that.'

'Well, good for Gloria.' I attempt to sound enthusiastic, but my grin is getting in the way.

'Good for her soul perhaps, but oh-so-bad for her soles,' he teases, even though his chest is puffed up with pride. Gloria may be Sam's adopted mum but they share a special love and a bond that could make a blind man see again.

Up ahead Mum and Mick have stopped at an old disfigured Ford which, although once originally painted metallic gold, has been dulled by time and a coastal climate to an uneven shade of stagnant pond water. The bumper is dented and unhinged at one end and there's a broad graze down the passenger side where Mick was once accosted by a wall at Tesco's. Still, I have reassuring memories of this car. When Sam had a panic attack at a protest march a few months ago it was this rusted ingot that carried him safely home again. I could never forget that day; it was probably the scariest of my life. Not only did I watch my lovely Sam rolling about wildly on the tarmac – his body rigor-mortis-rigid with fear, but I learned all about his tragic and strangely uplifting past and about Gloria's son, Adam. It was also on this day that I first fell in love with Sam and how I came to like him as much as I do now.

Sam is Samir Pejic – a Bosnian war orphan. Adam was Gloria's birth son who died ten years ago in that same war, even though he was British. Adam was nineteen years old when he went to Bosnia with the United Nations peacekeeping forces. And one day the humanitarian convoy he was leading into the capital Sarajevo was hit by a mortar shell. Adam was killed instantly. The grief nearly killed Gloria too. She was a single mum and Adam was her only child so, like Sam, she had also lost her entire family to the war. But she refused to be swallowed up by the sadness. She was determined to squeeze some good out of the bad and so she adopted Samir Pejic. Or Sam, as we've come to know and love him. He was only four years old at the time, but he still shares headspace with some of the memories.

'Are you hungry, Libby? Mick's made us chickpea burgers for lunch.' That was my mum's voice. The thoughts suddenly scatter and regroup around the subject of food. Yes, we're definitely hungry.

'Sounds good,' I reply and manage to unravel a smile. *Mick this, Mick that*. Still, the meal does sound vaguely appetising.

'I think a barbeque might be more fun.' Sam chuckles.

This makes me laugh out loud. It is good to be home.

There it is: her smell. My skin is instantly sticky with its chilled saltiness. I'm peering through the car window for a glimpse of her, but everybody knows that you always smell the ocean way before you see her. If I didn't love Mum and Sam as much as I do I'd still come here – just for her. I've never known anything quite so powerful and angry and wild yet peaceful and lazy. The great diva and her extravagant mood swings stoke my spirit and my senses, every single one of them. Today she's playful and striking; a flurry of blue-black energetic curls glinting with white crests that catch the pale winter sun every time she exposes herself this way and that. She doesn't want us to miss a thing. I'm so consumed by her show of clapping and cavorting that I don't even notice the building growing larger in the distance.

Mum may live on the outskirts of Brighton's sights and sounds but her colourful cottage is pinned to the ocean's sandy shoulder like an old and much-loved brooch. When the bleached Ford finally stops moving I'm the first one out. I embrace the ocean first, full on, and siphon her scent through long deep breaths until my lungs are full and my lips are cold, dry and salty. Only then do I turn to face the single storey cottage Mum shares with her New Age chum called Lotus.

'Come on Libby, Gloria and Lotus are dying to see you!' Mum bubbles enthusiastically.

'That's a bit drastic,' I joke. But I am really looking forward to seeing them too. Sam has my bag and is already making his way towards the front door and the sign that reads: *With the Power of Love Comes Peace in the World.* I follow his lead.

Once inside, the only thing that seems to have changed since my last visit is the air. It smells of chickpeas and patchouli. A second, closer inspection reveals one more difference: there's a small shiny Christmas tree decorating a corner of the front room. I absolutely know that this is for my benefit alone. Mum is 'spiritual, not religious'. And she 'doesn't believe in celebrating a religious holiday simply for the sake of it'. But otherwise everything else inside the cottage is just as I left it. I take a moment to absorb the warm interior glowing with soft lighting and creamy neutral colours. Mum and Lotus are Zen Minimalists, which means that they're only supposed to own what they really need. So there's a brown hessian rug to warm the wooden floor, a low-slung table made out of railway sleepers to rest things on, and scattered floor cushions covered in intricate embroidery and patchworks of shiny material to sit on. Mum and Lotus meditate in this room at least once a day. I don't suppose the garish glare of red and green tinsel and the view of the ever-present angel skewered by the tip of the fake Christmas tree helps their spiritual contemplation much.

'Hellooo,' Mum yodels into the chickpea air.

No answer.

'Where could they be?' Now she's less vocal; she seems to be talking to herself.

I'm also caught up in my own little world – or, more specifically, in the home I've missed so much. Nestled inside the belly of the cottage is the dining room with a fireplace and a round table surrounded by six upright chairs. But if you want to eat at this table you'll have to redirect the books, strewn papers, vials of essential oils and healing crystals jamming up its surface first. Still, Mum does make an effort to tidy when I'm around because this room is where I sleep when I visit. A short hard tug is all it takes to transform the couch in the corner into a very comfortable futon. I turn my back on the room and find Mum waving a bit of notepaper in the air.

'There was a problem at the Project,' she explains, 'Lotus and Gloria had to rush off. Shall we eat without them?'

I know all about the Project, full title The International Peace Project. Sam has kept me well informed over a series of emails. 'I don't mind waiting,' I shrug.

'Me neither,' Sam agrees. 'The Project office is close by. Why don't you and I take a walk over and say hello in the meantime?'

I've been anticipating my first visit for weeks. Of course I'd like to spend time with my mum too, but right now that time would include Mick. I nod enthusiastically. 'Good idea!'

'OK, you two head off and we'll finish getting lunch ready.' Mum kisses my forehead and disappears into the kitchen quickly followed by Mick. Sam throws me my still-warm jacket and we head out of the same door we entered not too long ago. Sifting the sudden onslaught of the ocean through my nostrils I wait patiently for Sam to pull up beside me. Only then do I set off walking. It's good to have him close again. It's bitterly cold out so our hands are tucked inside our jacket pockets for warmth. Still, there's no hurry. Electric sparks flare and fly about every time our elbows collide.

'It's good to have you back again, Liberty Belle,' Sam smiles.

'It's really good to be back.' There's so much more I could add, but with Sam I don't have to. He knows exactly how I feel. So I ask him about school and life in general instead.

'We've started vocational classes,' he reveals, adding, 'to help us decide what we want to do with our lives.'

'You mean like what job you want to do?'

'And what subjects we want to study. I think I'd like to do some sort of work that involves the ocean.' Now he turns his head and looks at me with a broad grin. His eyes meet mine; he knows that this is exactly what I want to do too.

'We could get matching marine biologist badges?' I suggest and then laugh.

'You could be my assistant.'

'Fat chance!' I take this opportunity to bump him with my hip. Just then a scooter roars past. 'I've started saving up for one of those,' I admit and jerk a thumb at the fading sound. 'Of course my father would haemorrhage if he found out but once I'm old enough and legal…and besides, I'll need my independence.'

'But where would I fit?' Sam asks.

'You'll have to buy your own scooter. You can follow

behind me.' Sam laughs and it's in this way that we walk while we talk about the rest of the little things that have some significance in our lives. And before long the row of shops Mum would be lost without (they stock all the essentials, and then some) looms into view.

Sam comes to a sudden stop. 'Would you mind if I quickly popped into For Old Times' Sake?'

I know that shop, although I've never been inside. It sells antiques. 'Course not.' I shake my head vigorously.

'I won't be a moment – you wait here.' He smiles mysteriously and then quickly disappears inside the shop.

'But I'll come with—' The door swings shut in my face. That's not like Sam. Mmm, the thoughts muse. He soon re-emerges, clutching a small parcel carefully wrapped in natural brown paper and tied with gold raffia. It looks so pretty.

'What's that?'

'You'll find out later, it's a surprise. Now come on.' Sam pulls me by the arm and uses the motion to hook his elbow through mine. And that's how we continue walking along the pavement, arm in arm, with shops facing us on both sides and a cold ocean smell in our nostrils. I'm so caught up in the moment I don't even notice the girl with pale brown skin until she's less than ten metres away from us. She looks to be about sixteen years old – a little older than us – and she's standing outside a department store with a small stack of magazines in her hand. She's dressed in a long loose beige skirt and a thick woollen zip-up cardigan. On her dark head is a black scarf that covers her hair entirely and falls in soft folds beneath her chin before disappearing inside the collar of her cardigan. She's calling out to people as they pass but I can't make out her words.

At that moment three pale lads with short-shaven heads and wearing hoodies exit the shop's double-doors and swagger onto the pavement. We're getting closer. I estimate that they're younger than us, probably about twelve years old or so. I notice them looking at the girl with the black headscarf.

'*Big Issue*,' calls the girl to a mother pushing a buggy. She has an accent I don't recognise – it might be East European. The mother ignores her, even though she probably knows that *The Big Issue* is a magazine sold by people living on the streets and in hostels who are trying to make a better life for themselves.

One of the hoodies nudges his mates. They all snigger.

'Oi, what's the headscarf for?' This time it's a lad with bright white new-looking trainers demanding attention.

'Come on girl, let's have a look at you,' one of the other boys chimes in. Another mate, wearing a gold hoop earring, suddenly makes a grab for the girl's scarf. She steps back and manages to dodge his fingers. It's for religious reasons that she's never seen out in public without her headscarf. She looks alarmed. The brazen boy is frightening her.

'Forget the hair, show us some skin,' New Trainers shouts with a hand cupped around his mouth. Now he's laughing maniacally.

'Yeah, you Muslim girls think you're sumfink special so you gotta cover it all up, do ya? I got a mate who did it with a Muslim. He told me she went at it like a—'

Sam suddenly yanks his arm from mine and tilts forward to take off. He doesn't even have to update me – I'm right beside him, tensed up and poised to sprint. But we're not quick enough. A bald man dressed in a dreary grey suit pinned with a name badge that says *Sid Brunswick, Manager* strides out of the store's double-doors and reaches the lads before we do.

'Oi, you lot, clear off before I call the cops!' he shouts at the three hoodies. They laugh at him but quickly amble off, away from the girl and storefront. Sid Brunswick, Manager then faces the girl. 'And you – get lost. I don't want to see you here again.' He turns from her, muttering as he disappears back through the double-doors. 'All trouble, the lot of ya...'

The expression on the face of the girl in the headscarf shows a mixture of fearful pride. Her lips are white and straight, as if she's working hard at keeping them closed. But her eyes are wide and anxious. She glances at us briefly and then instantly turns on her heel and strides away, always facing forward and keeping her head tilted slightly upwards.

I can't help staring at her shrinking form. 'That was awful,' I finally whisper. Inside my head the thoughts are raging. And the one question they keep repeating over and over is *why, why, why*? What did those boys gain from being so mean? They resent her because she's not exactly like them, and now she resents them and probably thinks that other white kids are just like them too. And she'll go and tell others like her, who might now also feel resentment just like her. Those boys just set hate in motion. And one day we'll all hate everybody, but we won't be quite sure why. 'Don't we realise how much damage we can do to one another?' I wonder out loud.

Sam sighs. 'Some people don't care.' He's also still staring at the girl.

'Maybe making other people feel bad makes them

feel better…or bigger?'

Sam nods his head and kicks something imaginary on the ground. 'Some people are ignorant and insecure and can't accept anybody who doesn't look, sound and believe just like them.'

Now I'm thinking about Sam's family – not Gloria, but his birth family who were killed. How did this happy day turn out so gloomy? I desperately don't want my first day in Brighton with Sam to be like this.

'Come on, it's all over now. So how about you let me see what's inside the package?' I'm grinning mischievously and pointing to the brown paper parcel tied up with gold raffia.

Sam quickly yanks it up high over his head and out of my reach. 'Nope. I said you'll have to wait. And besides, we'd better get moving.'

So I don't get to see my gift, but at least our moods have lifted. We set off down the pavement and leave the department store, Sid Brunswick, Manager and the bad memory behind us.

'Saaam!' a voice calls out. We both turn in its direction. Now the voice is silent and, of course, I don't recognise anyone, but Sam seems to. He raises his right arm and waves at the group of kids loitering a short distance away.

'Come on Libby, let me introduce you to some of my friends.'

For a brief moment I'm glued to the ground, my head a mad buzzing, whirring jumble of talking thoughts. *I really don't want to meet Sam's other friends because I'll just feel like the odd one out and they're probably more fun than me which means he might want to hang out with them even though this is meant to be our time and chances are they might not even like me not that I care, I'm Sam's friend. Course I knew he had others but I don't want to meet them I'll just say the wrong things and sound stupid oh why oh why didn't we just stay home with Mum and Chicken Mick!*

'Libby?'

'Uh, yeah sure.' I stumble along beside him, staring at the looming group of kids with fearful anticipation. There are three boys – two of them carrying skateboards – and one girl. She's about my height with bobbed brown hair and is dressed in jeans and a puffy pink parka. Yes, she's definitely a girl. I notice her looking me up and down too.

'Hi guys,' Sam greets the group. There's a commotion as they execute three-point handshakes in typical bloke style. The Girl, meanwhile, flicks her eyes between Sam and me and chews gum.

'Do you remember I told you about Libby?' Sam touches my arm as he says this. I watch The Girl's eyes drop to my arm and then settle back on my face again. Chew chew.

'Greetings.' One of the boys smiles and gives a friendly salute.

'Hey there,' says another.

'Hiya.'

The Girl doesn't say anything but she does give me a watery smile. Everyone seems quite friendly. Still, I wish we weren't standing here. Or I wish they weren't standing there, I'm flexible either way…

'So are you enjoying Brighton?' one of the boys asks.

I nod and smile. I'm too nervous to trust my vocal chords right now.

'Pity you have to spend your time here with the Sameister though, huh,' another boy chuckles good-naturedly and slaps Sam on the back.

'Yeah, life can be cruel sometimes. Ha ha,' laughs another.

Sam smiles too. 'You're a funny guy, Johnno.'

I still haven't spoken. I'm quietly watching my best friend, the one I call my soul mate, mingling in his world. This is his natural environment. He's relaxed and amused; these are obviously good friends. I should be glad for him. Instead I'm grumpy and intimidated and jealous and feeling sorry for myself.

'We're all heading to the Skate Pit,' reveals the boy Sam just called Johnno. 'Are you coming along?'

Sam turns to me and I try my very best to keep my face empty. Of course I don't want to go – I'd rather drink a snot-vomit milkshake. But I don't want to make Sam feel uncomfortable or stand between him and his friends either. I love him too much to do that. So I simply try to keep my face blank and hope that he'll reach the right decision (or my version thereof, anyway) all on his own. The seconds pass like hours. I can feel The Girl's eyes on me again. The sound of cars passing is a long, decelerated *whoosh* in my ears. Sam is still staring at me. If he's expecting some sort of visual clue he's wasting his time; I'm keeping the face bare. I don't want to pressurise him, but I'm not just handing over our afternoon to his friends either.

'Uh, thanks all the same,' he finally replies, 'but we've really got to get going. We're expected home for lunch.'

Suddenly time returns to its normal tick-tock pace. The cars speed up once again and zoom past us in a blur while I shrug and smile at everyone and no one in particular.

'No worries,' replies Johnno with a smile and a nod. 'Give us a call and we'll meet up sometime soon then.'

Sam grins. 'Definitely.'

'Nice to meet you all,' I finally speak. I then give a small wave, to show that I really mean it, too. Now that my personal crisis is over I suppose I really do want them to like me. They all say goodbye, even The Girl, and we go our separate ways. But I don't talk again until there are at least six shops between Sam and me and them. 'They seem really nice,' I say.

'Yup, they are.' He nods but doesn't add anything further. Just like a boy.

'So who's the girl?'

'That's Simone – she's Johnno's sister.' Silence. I can hear birds chirruping; he's obviously not going to give me any further information.

'Ooooh right,' I say with keen interest, like I just discovered that the sun is actually a star or that polar bears are left-handed. 'She seems nice.'

'Yup, she is.' Chirp. Chirp.

'So are you and The Girl – I mean Simone, quite good friends then?'

Sam turns slowly to face me. Now he's grinning. 'You're not jealous are you, Liberty Belle?'

'Oh please! *AS IF!*' I make a face like I had just drunk that snot-vomit milkshake. What a freakish suggestion.

Sam is still laughing at me. 'Come on, we're late.'

'There it is.' Sam finally points to an unimpressive pale concrete box-shaped building up ahead. He then looks at me and smiles, guessing that I'm thinking it's not up to much. 'Someone loaned us the office space, free of charge. We are a charity, after all.'

'Exactly! And what's a building anyway,' I reply quickly. Betrayed by the face again, the thoughts scowl. I could kick my shallow self. But really I can't wait to be involved; I want to help make a difference. And I'm just in time too. The International Peace Project is a worldwide peace movement determined to spread the message of peace, love and acceptance. And the special day they've chosen to do this is New Year's Day, which is only sixteen days away.

Sam explained that there is a group of International Peace Project volunteer organisers stationed in every single country around the world. My geography is a bit vague so I had to ask: apparently there are 193. Countries, that is. The idea is to send a prayer for peace across the entire planet, starting in Chile, the southernmost country in the world, then crisscrossing the entire globe and finally ending in Iceland – the northernmost country. The first prayer will begin at 12.01 am GMT on the 1st of January and the prayer will be passed along every seven minutes from that moment onwards. The entire event has been carefully calculated and orchestrated so that by the end of the first day of the New Year the entire world will be blessed by a prayer for peace. It will filter through every country, infusing the air and hearts and minds of its people with thoughts of harmony and love. Even if I had a hundred lifetimes to live over, I still don't think I could come up with a better way to begin a brand new year.

The Peace Project office is at the rear of the building, which appears to be used for storage by a company that sells pet accessories over the internet. Otherwise the building is deserted. Sam leads me down a corridor to an unmarked door. It opens with a faint creak; disused rooms rarely have well-oiled door hinges. The air inside is hot and stuffy. And there's Gloria and Lotus, looking hot and stuffy.

'I can't locate the thermostat—' Lotus groans, spying Sam at the door. 'Libby!' She's just noticed me lurking behind Sam. 'Liberty Belle, come over here right this minute!' I do as I'm told, covered in a sheepish smile;

I know where this is heading. Lotus suctions a hand to either side of my head and pulls my face towards her own. She then covers me in a flurry of kisses, finally ending on my forehead, where she lingers the longest. 'Oh, we have missed you. It's just gorgeous to see you again!' she gushes grandly.

There's nothing half-mast about our Lotus. 'I've missed you too.' I sound dismal and diluted by comparison, but I really mean it.

'Hello Libby.' That's Gloria, and she's smiling at me fondly too. I don't know her very well, but I know her well enough.

'Hi there, Gloria.' I move to give her a warm hug because that's what you do in my mum's world. Plus I really like Gloria. And she's Sam's mum, the thoughts add.

Both women take turns asking me about my journey from Manchester and my life in general and I respond with a few vague, summarised replies. I'm a teenager, they're not expecting much more information from me. And besides, I really just want to hear about the Peace Project.

'So what's the crisis that delayed lunch?' Sam finally asks.

'Oh, number seventy-eight in the peace prayer

chain – one of the island countries – almost withdrew. They're short of volunteers.'

'And interest, it would seem.' Lotus sighs and shakes her head sadly, like she'll never understand why not everyone cares about world peace like she does.

'Peace Project Montenegro did some super-smooth talking though,' Gloria joins in the explanation, gesturing to the PC on the desk. I assume this means that the super-smooth talking was done via email. 'And they managed to get the little island to climb aboard the peace train once more. Ha ha.'

Lotus joins in. 'Ha ha.'

That's New Age humour. Even if I do get the joke, I rarely keel over laughing.

'That's great.' Sam grins. He's just as happy and passionate about the Project as Lotus and Gloria. 'Destination: Peaceville!'

'Choo choo,' I add in a small shy voice, eager to be part of the group. I've been dodging dumbbells in Manchester; I just need some time to catch up, that's all.

'This is the map I was telling you about, Libby,' Sam explains, pointing to the giant map of the world taped to the wall. I move closer and stare at its continents diced up by lines of longitude and latitude. There's Italy – the boot. There's the equator. Ah, and Iceland.

The map is also pocked with tiny handwritten numbers wrapped up in circles. In some cases a lack of space means that certain countries have arrows pointing to the number-filled circles. The map is certainly busy.

'See, this is the trail the prayer for peace will take,' Sam continues, tracing a finger from one number to the next. So number one must be Chile, I reason while I search. My eyes have trekked south but I still haven't found Chile or number one. No wonder I never achieved anything better than a C for geography. Still, I did stumble upon Iceland. Luckily Sam seems oblivious to my stupidity. 'The organisers for each country are very busy co-ordinating a mass assembly of people to pray for peace. They will meet at a scheduled location in their country on New Year's Day and recite the prayer at their particular allocated time.'

'We've contacted a few British TV stations; we may even get live coverage,' Gloria reveals excitedly.

'Actually we're hoping that TV stations all around the world will cover the Peace Project gathering in their particular country,' Lotus adds with her eyebrows pulled all the way up to her hairline while her hands shimmy in the air. 'It should be absolutely magnificent. Let peace reign eternal!' She used to be a drama teacher before she gave it all up for peace. This rarely surprises people.

'It all sounds really great,' I cheer, resting my smile on Lotus first, then Gloria and finally on my best friend, who is standing there looking content and inspired and just as lovely as the picture of him I hold fast in my mind's eye.

Lotus is the one to break the moment. 'There's lunch waiting for us and we're all done here – so let's get going. I'm just famished!' We all nod and immediately carry ourselves to the door and off home where there's warm food and more friendly faces waiting.

During lunch I sit between Mum and Sam at the dining-room table that's right beside the couch that transforms into a futon. I'm going to be dreaming about chickpea burgers tonight. Still, they are better than Lotus's tofu quiche or Mum's seaweed and lentil fajitas. Mick doesn't say very much during lunch (or ever, really – as far as I can tell) so it's fairly easy to pretend that he's not the other bookend keeping Mum upright. Or it was, until everyone started slapping him on the back and praising his cooking skills, which meant that I should follow suit. It would be too obvious not to. So I did. 'Thanks for lunch, Mick,' I said.

'No problem,' he replied and then subtly tickled my mum's hand with his pinkie finger.

Chicken legs, chickpea head Mick! That was the talking thoughts, honest.

'How about we all take a stroll along the beach?' Sam suggests. He knows how much I miss the ocean.

'Sounds great.' I nod.

'I think we're too old to brave the winter chill

needlessly, sweetheart. But you two run along,' Mum replies with a smirk. She then gives the others a big fat wink. She knows Sam and I have a lot of catching up to do; she obviously thinks she's doing us a favour by giving us some alone time. Which is nice, except the woman is about as subtle as street lighting at Christmas. Mick is also grinning and winking and beaming like a six-foot illuminated Santa.

'Yes, it's definitely way too cold out there.' Gloria gives a mock shiver.

'And I am just bushed!' That was Lotus.

Sam suddenly opens his mouth before I can. 'Right, well we're off then.' He knows me too well.

As the brisk outside air hits my exposed cheeks, my warmed pink complexion quickly transforms to a chilled ruby. But I don't mind the cold – it's just so good to be near the ocean with my best friend at my side and my mum just a bit further away.

'So I've taken up fishing,' Sam reveals as he falls in step with me.

Thanks to email, Sam and I manage to remain up to date and tell each other everything. Or so I thought. 'Oh, really?' I smile, lacing my elbow through his. 'First bodybuilding, now fishing. What's next, Samir Pejic?'

'I am a man of many skills, there is nothing I can't manage or master.'

'Is that so?' I laugh out loud. 'I have one word, three syllables for you, mister: ka-ra-oke.' I've heard Sam sing and the pain is physical.

'Everyone's a critic.' He sniffs the cold air and then drags me even closer with his elbow. 'But I have got the fishing thing taped. I've even entered Brighton's Best fishing tournament. It's in a few weeks' time – I've been practising my casting like a madman. See those groynes out there?' His outstretched finger is pointing in the direction of a pair of low, broad concrete walls built at right angles to the sea wall and projecting out into the ocean.

I follow his gaze beyond the beach with its joggers and fellow ocean lovers out walking their dogs or legs. I see the walls and nod my head like a good A-grade student. 'Uh huh.'

'The purpose of the groynes is to trap shingle and create a defence ahead of the sea wall. And at low tide they're also superb for fishing off,' he adds brightly. '*That's* where the casting magic happens.'

'A groyne and a fishing rod, what more could a person ask for?' *Sigh.* I can't even pretend to sound interested.

'Come on, I'll give you a tour. You might be in for a pleasant surprise.'

I very much doubt it, but I let Sam-Sam-the-fisherman take me to the steps that lead down to the pebble beach anyway. En-route we pass a large noticeboard printed with four little pictures encased in four faded yellow triangles, each with a warning printed beneath: Beware Deep-Shelving Beach; Beware Kite Surfing; Beware Large Breaking Waves; and Beware Submerged Objects. A neighbouring noticeboard features four red circles with pictures and some *do nots* written below each one: Do Not Dive; Do Not Jump; Do Not Swim; Do Not Use Inflatables. The noticeboard concludes with big red letters that warn: Caution – This Beach Is Not Lifeguarded. The news is not surprising – this is hardly *Baywatch* territory, the talking thoughts observe.

With the steps behind us we're now level with the ocean and I can feel her wet, salty breath seasoning my skin, leaving a residue that will dry to a fine white powder.

'You're not cold, are you?' Sam's hand is reaching for mine.

I shake my head and concentrate on my footing. Walking along this uneven beach of smooth mottled pebbles is four-by-fouring for feet. Sam's warm hand is firm in mine; he's doing his best to support me while I adapt to the shifting stones underfoot. That's just one of the things I love about Sam – he's always looking out for me. For each and every pebble lying on this beach today there's a reason for loving Sam. I probably wouldn't even know where to begin listing each one. OK, so he's smart, he can make me laugh at just about anything (especially myself), he always puts others first, he's tall and brown with dark hair that curls just enough to be wild and beautiful, he's got towering piles of interesting information stored up in his head, he's cool but always just that little bit different from everyone else, he's got a laugh that can make your day...

'You know at high tide it's almost impossible to reach these groynes.'

More talk of groynes. *Groan.* And I was just thinking such lovely talking thoughts.

'They're mostly submerged at high tide,' Sam continues, gesturing to the waves and the broad concrete wall washed dark brown by the water. 'But at low tide,' he grins at me, 'you can safely walk out along them just far enough to catch some pretty decent-sized fish.'

'Very smart.' I smile back, trying to fan his flames. He obviously loves those fish. And I love Sam, which is why I'm going to love those fish too. It's the mathematics of love.

'Ha, it wasn't my idea – fishermen have been fishing off these groynes since forever. Well, ever since they were built, anyway.'

'Great.' It's all I can think of to say. I was only trying to feel love for the fish.

'I want to show you my favourite fishing spot, but first…' If I didn't know any better I'd say that Sam suddenly looks nervous. 'But first I want to give you this.' He releases my hand and loses it to his pocket. It quickly re-emerges holding the parcel wrapped in natural brown paper tied up with gold raffia.

'What is it?'

'You're meant to open it and find out.' He grins at me. 'I know your birthday is only tomorrow but, well, consider this the starter course of birthday gifts. I wanted to give it to you while we're alone.' I don't say anything and simply stare at the pretty gift wrapping. 'Plus this is the best place, if any, to give it to you,' he quickly adds, sounding slightly breathless. Come to think of it, he's almost rambling. 'Go on, open it – you'll see.'

I do as I'm told and very soon I'm holding a small, flat wooden case just a little bigger than my palm. The top of the case is set with two round circles of glass that look like spectacle lenses. My fingers touch a little brass clasp and the lid releases. Inside the case is a stack of small black and white postcards printed with seaside images. I can tell they're seaside images, but each one seems slightly out of focus, as if there's a shadow of itself slightly off centre.

'Here, let me show you.' Sam slides the case from my grip and deftly releases two metal hinges that prop the lid of the case open. He then pops a small piece of notched wood into a slot so that it's standing upright. Now I see how it works. The wood holds the postcards in place so that they're standing vertical and positioned directly in front of the lenses.

'Look through the glass.' Again, I do as I'm told. The postcards are suddenly and miraculously transformed into spectacular three-dimensional images of the seaside. There are bobbing boats, their sails filled-to-bursting with the breeze, seagulls diving beak-first into the high-tipped ocean, and beaches washed smooth and glistening by the churning waves. Looking through the lenses, I'm overwhelmed by the sudden and very strange sensation that I've *entered* the postcards. It's like I'm actually there, floating amongst the seagulls and waves and boats with puffed-out sails.

'Wow!' I gasp.

'Cool, huh?' Sam is smiling, delighted by my reaction. 'It's a Victorian stereograph – a three-dimensional postcard viewer. What's really amazing is that when you look through the lenses it's like actually being *inside* the images! I saw it in the antique shop a while ago, and when I saw the seaside postcards I knew I had to get it for you. This way, whenever you miss the ocean, all you have to do is gaze through the stereograph lenses.'

Now if only I had a blurry postcard of Sam and my mum. 'It's absolutely wonderful. Thank you, Sam. I'll treasure it.'

'I'm glad you like it. Now come on.' He hoists himself up onto the flat broad ledge of the groyne and then kneels down to offer me his hand. I really would have been happy with the long-distance tour but if I want to share in Sam's world and love the fish then I must get involved. I return the stereograph to its bag and bury it safely inside the zippered pocket of my jacket. Then wedging the toe of my trainer into a rut in the groyne's concrete side and using one hand for leverage, I almost manage to scale the wall without looking too ridiculously girly. And the move really might have gone smoothly, if only Sam hadn't used all his strength to hoist me up. The end result is that I land right on top of him, pointy knees, winter chubby bits and all. It wasn't the look I was going for.

'Eugh!' He doesn't say anything else; I may have winded the boy.

'Oh, I'm hardly that heavy!' I squawk defensively, quickly jumping off his ribs and dusting my hands off daintily. 'And you shouldn't have pulled so hard.'

'Of course not,' he finally groans and crawls to his feet. 'Now come along, Your Nimbleness, we've got a wall to explore.' And with that he begins his trek across the flat ledge of the groyne, peering down its sheer sides every so often as he walks. I follow closely and make an effort to peer where he's peering (because that's how you go about looking interested).

'Some ocean creatures,' he finally speaks again, 'can thrive in exposed conditions. Look there.' He's pointing to the outcrop of rocks packed against the groyne's side. 'Those cone-shaped shells clamped tightly to the rocks are limpets. And those darker, smaller lumps are acorn barnacles – a type of crustacean. You don't want to land on those; they'll give you a nasty graze.' He gives me a mischievous grin. 'Now lean over carefully and focus on the crannies in the concrete.'

I do as I'm told. I think I'm meant to be looking at the red and green jelly-like blobs growing out of the wall's narrow eroded cracks.

'Those are beadlet anemones,' Sam declares authoritatively and then widens his search, carefully inspecting the water lapping at the groyne. 'See how they huddle close together?'

I nod like an enthralled student held under the hypnotising spell of my tutor. 'Uh huh.'

Sam gives me a little smirk and pulls me towards him. 'Well, move in closer.' I do as I'm told and bask in Sam's body heat while he continues the tour.

'You used to get a lot of periwinkles in the more sheltered areas, but they're good to eat so their numbers have dwindled.'

I really don't have to feign interest any more; this is fascinating and rather romantic stuff! I usually think of the ocean as a great diva, but she's really so much more. Sam says that she's an ecosystem – a self-contained world with complex food chains and organisms that have adapted to extreme and unusual conditions. She's also home to the smallest plankton and the largest creature on earth, the blue whale. But even better is that a love for the ocean is something both Sam and I share, and it brings us even closer.

'Come along,' Sam urges me on enthusiastically, 'I'll show you my favourite fishing spot.'

This time I reach for Sam's hand. Now we're one

again. He leads me further along the wall's ledge and for a moment it feels like we're walking on water. Or maybe that's just more of Sam's magic. All around us silver-green waves clamber and tumble about, pulled and pushed by the deeper currents surging and swirling out of sight. Every so often a crowd of waves gather in a line and then race for the land, shattering themselves gleefully against the pebbled shore before regrouping and rolling back out to the backline, ready to start a brand new race all over again. When Sam finally stops walking there's about three metres of wall ledge remaining in front of us. If we want to go any further after that then we really will have to walk on water.

'This is it.' He's stomping his feet gleefully on the spot, casting and reeling in an imaginary fishing rod. 'This is where it happens – the casting magic that's sure to win me first prize.'

'You look like a natural.' I smile. 'You'll definitely have to take me fishing sometime soon.' And I mean it too. Unlike the fish, I think I might like it.

But Sam doesn't seem to be listening to me. He's pretending that he's hooked me and reeling himself in closer. 'I don't think I'll be putting *you* back,' he says. He grins down at me and then swaps the imaginary fishing rod for my flesh-and-bone shoulders. I forgot to mention Sam's hugs; there's just nothing to beat them.

'Yeah, I am a bit of a catch.' I'm trying to sound flippant but inside I'm like one of those anemones – all wobbly jelly.

'I couldn't agree more.' But that's all he says, because suddenly his lips are kissing mine, gently – over and over, like soft drops of warm rain in a tropical storm. I stand there, stock still, with my head tilted to heaven and my arms hanging limply at my sides, soaking it all up. The sensation is overwhelming and I am officially mesmerised and incapable until further notice. Sam's downpour of kisses waters my dehydrated soul until it's ballooned to just-about-bursting. And only when my heart is filled to capacity do I finally begin to feel the stirrings of life and my senses returning to me.

Sam's arms are holding me firm and I reach around his back and curl in tighter for more of his closeness. All around us the cold ocean air is being blown about by a strong breeze and buffeting our single, solitary shape at the end of the groyne. Inside I'm smiling; it's one more reason to hold on tightly to Sam. I stopped feeling cold some time ago too; right now I could probably melt a polar icecap if we came too close. My lips are tingling and sweet with the taste of our kisses. I can't think past this moment and right now feels like forever. Sam's hand has begun tracing the shape of my—

Suddenly I'm hit from behind. The wall is cold and hard – a sheet of ice smashing and shattering against my spine and the back of my skull. It knocks me forward and I collide with Sam for the second time today. But this time we don't fall to the ground. The space around us is rushing with foam and bubbles that seem determined to climb inside my nose and lungs. Every part of me is wet and burning. I'm pedalling uselessly; there's no floor for my feet. I'm being swept out to sea; the powerful tide is dragging me farther and farther away from the groyne and the beach and into deeper water. It's like I'm caught in a washing machine's spin cycle – being whooshed this way and that. I drag my screaming eyes through the waves. Sam has vanished from my arms. *Where is he!* I'm trying desperately to grab for him with my fingers but the force around me is too much. Then the thought disappears. Now all I can think about is how much my body frantically craves air.

My release is abrupt and unexpected. The great old diva has tired of me – her dreary, washed-out plaything. When I finally bob to the surface the water around me is smoother and less agitated, but I barely notice. I must breathe. I rise out of the waves like a creature from the deep – with my jaws wide open, straining painfully for oxygen. At first there's a vacuum of nothingness and then all of a sudden an immense gush of air surges down my windpipe. The sound of scraping fills my head and is quickly followed by a great gasp that rattles the back of my throat and every bone in my body. But I am alive, that much I'm almost sure of.

Sam? *'Sam!'* I manage to scream his name but the wind throws it back in my face like my efforts aren't good enough. Of course I'm searching the water around me but the waves seem like mountains. No matter which way I turn I can only see peaks of water rising and melting in front of me. I may as well be blind. Even the groyne has disappeared.

My invisible legs are cutting the water and keeping my head afloat. With a little more effort I could probably expose my shoulders too; it's the only way I might be able to see further. So, sculling rhythmically with my palms open beside me, I use everything I have inside me to bring my legs together in one short, snappy movement. And it works. I bob at least ten inches higher out of the icy water, but still there's nothing but waves. Silently praying that I'm facing the horizon and that the shore is waiting patiently behind me I scull 180 degrees and, summoning up my reserve of strength,

I repeat the leg movement. And there it is – the beach with people out walking their dogs and legs! They're looking in my direction too. Now they're waving. I pull one hand from sculling duty and wave back frantically.

'HELP ME!' I scream so loud that my strained voice is nothing more than a whimper. Undeterred, I try once more, only this time I'm less violent with my vocal chords. My reward is a cry that second-time-around seems so much louder in my ears. My heart swears that my howl has not gone unheard, but my head is less optimistic. Still, the people with the dogs must know that I'm here, surely. Why else would they be waving? I've got brain freeze; I can't think clearly.

All of a sudden there's movement to my right. *Sam?* There's something yellow but it's still a way off. Now I see it clearly. It's not my missing friend. There's a rubber duck riding the waves. And it's heading my way. Perhaps they have Sam already. The thought warms me slightly, but still I'm so cold I can barely manage to keep my numb limbs moving. I'm losing the connection to my arms and legs and my joints are starting to seize up. I must focus on the boat instead. Every so often a wave surprises me and slaps me across the face, a cold contemptuous hand mocking me for being out where I plainly don't belong. *Silly girl, what were you thinking – turning your back on the diva!* I'm crying but that's good because my tears are diluting the salty ocean lapping at my eyes. Just then a pitying wave hoists me to its curling crest and I spy the boat once more. It's hardly moving at all. Now the only way I can keep myself afloat is by thinking about Sam sitting in that warm, dry boat, never taking his eyes off me for an instant. I always said he was a lifesaver.

eight
hell's gate

I don't really remember being rescued. I do recall feeling apprehensive as the rubber duck approached – I felt certain that it was going to mow me down. But then I saw that Sam wasn't inside the boat after all, and then I really didn't mind if I was ocean kill. I figured that at least then I'd be a link in the ocean's food chain; my life would still have some meaning. I might be seagull snacks or a bite-size shark treat, but I'd be doing my bit for the environment. Sam told me all about the ocean ecosystem, and I hadn't forgotten.

I spent one night in hospital under observation and woke the next morning to see my mum's face, peering down closely at me. Her eyes were creased with concern. I assured her that I felt fine – physically anyway – and manoeuvred myself upright on soft white hospital pillows. There were two other beds in my ward and neither of them held Sam safe and sound. So I asked Mum; I wanted to hear about Sam. Where was he? At first she tried to soothe and distract with me phrases like 'just take it easy' and 'try to get some rest' and 'there's nothing you can do for the moment', but I was having none of it. I screamed so loud she soon feared not telling me even more.

'Liberty, I'm so sorry darling – Sam is missing,' Mum finally revealed.

'Sam is missing,' I repeated, like saying the words out loud might help me to understand them better. *Sam has been missing since yesterday, when a rogue wave – whatever that is – swatted us off the groyne where we were kissing and clinging to one another like our lives depended on it.* I thought about this for a while. And then all I wanted to do was to be alone. I wanted to swat away Mum's concern and wallow in my sadness. Alone.

And so they sent me home this morning. I'm not fixed, but what could they really do for me? All the medicine in the world couldn't mend this broken-down heart. They gave Mum tablets to help me sleep. At first I dreamt of nothing but waves. I even felt nauseous, like my bed was rocking and rolling with the currents. Then I thought I heard Sam calling out for me. But now I just doze, suspended in a comfortable sedation – like I'm floating just below the surface of the truth. I'm aware of everything and everyone around me, but there's a thin blurry film softening reality's sharper edges that might otherwise just tear me to shreds.

Now I'm awake and in Mum's bed. There's nobody else in the bedroom and I'm relieved to find myself alone for the very first time since my rescue. I need some quiet time to think. Up until now Mum hasn't left my side.

My outward gaze is focussed on nothing in particular; everything is happening inside my head. I'm autopsying that precise moment over and over – the moment the wave smacked us apart with its firm icy backhand. I'm prising the details apart, studying each piece and then putting them back together again, but still the details remain slippery and vague. One minute Sam and I were locked in each other's arms, and then came the wave to tear us apart. It all happened so quickly.

Just then Mum enters the room. 'Oh, you're awake, sweetheart,' she observes with a small soothing smile.

'I should have kept a tighter hold on Sam,' I whisper hoarsely.

Suddenly Mum is at my bedside. 'What did you say, darling?'

'I should have kept a tighter hold on Sam!'

'Oh honey, you could never have held on to him, no matter how strong you were or how hard you tried,' Mum replies. Her face is serious and she's attempting to hook my gaze but I won't have any of it. Mums say things like that because it's their job to make you feel better.

For a while neither of us speaks. I'm feeling anger and grief; Mum looks uncomfortable, as if she's trying to make a life decision. Finally she puts her thoughts into words. 'There are two police officers here. They want to ask you some routine questions. I said I wasn't sure if you were up to it.' She looks at me expectantly.

'What for?' I wonder.

'They said you might be able to help with the investigation.'

I think this through seriously for a moment. So they're calling it an investigation. 'What are they going to do, arrest the wave?'

'It's just routine, darling. I'll tell them to come back tomorrow, or the next day.'

'No no, I'm fine.' Or course I must do everything possible to help find Sam. And so I trail Mum to the lounge where two police officers, one man and one woman, are waiting patiently.

They're smiling kindly and speak to me in soft, soothing tones. They want me to remember what happened. That's easy, remembering is all I've been doing. So I tell them everything I have inside my head about that terrible day. The woman nods and writes, the man asks questions every so often. I finish my story and think that's the end of it but the man wants me to start all the way from the beginning again, just to confirm a few details.

I look him straight in the eye and breathe deeply. 'Don't you think your time might be better spent *actually looking for Sam?*' I suggest.

I know he's out there. After all, he's only missing. People go missing every single day. I know this because I saw a documentary on telly about missing people. Most of them turn up, too. And Sam's a good swimmer. He's probably washed up somewhere but has amnesia and can't remember who or where he is.

'We are looking for Sam,' the policeman replies with his eyes resting heavily on mine. 'We have a land and sea search and rescue underway. They spent hours out there yesterday and the search has resumed again this morning.'

I suddenly don't want to talk to the man anymore. I don't want to hear about their land and sea search and rescue efforts. So everyone is out looking for Sam – and has been for hours and hours and hours and hours. And still they haven't found him anywhere. What good is that news to my ears?

Instead I turn to the woman. 'So just what exactly is a rogue wave?' I ask.

'A rogue wave is a relatively large and spontaneous ocean surface wave,' she repeats confidently. I had already asked Mum the same question but she wasn't entirely sure of the answer. I suspect that up until yesterday this policewoman really didn't know what it was either. But they have eyewitnesses – the people with legs and dogs walking on the beach. Some of them saw it happen.

Remembering that I want to do all I can to help find Sam I take a deep breath and once again begin retelling our story – the story of Sam and me and the last time we were together. I recollect walking along the groyne… the beadlet anenomes and acorn barnacles…Sam's imaginary fishing rod…and finally the wave. But I know very little about the wave; it came from behind. Finally the police officers look satisfied.

'Thanks, love,' the woman says.

'Take care now,' the man concludes and tips his hat gently before heading for the front door of the cottage. I remain seated and let Mum see them out.

'How about a cup of tea?' she asks when she returns.

'No thanks,' I reply, 'I'm off to look for Sam.' I put my weight on my feet on the floor. I stand up and then I fall down again. My pointy knees, just like my heart, are obviously broken. Mum rushes over to me and tries to help me up. But I just want to sit here, on the floor. I just want to sit on the floor and cry. The soft cushions are too good for me.

The tears come quick and fall fast, sliding down my face like sweat and plopping on my broken knees like hot heavy beads. I am shaking from the inside out, shivering with uncontrollable grief and pain. *Where is my Sam who survived a war but couldn't survive a wave?* Sorrow grips my chest and my throat and I cry till I burn. I cry until I feel empty. I then cry and cry some more. But still the misery is there, consuming me from the inside out.

'Darling?'

If I keep very still the voice might go away.

'Darling, are you awake?'

So much for that theory. I reluctantly prise one lid open and wait an unsettled moment for my eyes to slowly find their focus button. I'm still in Mum's bed and there's a face only inches from my own. It's my mum and she's smiling gently while rhythmically combing her fingers through my pillow hair, over and over.

'It's six o'clock, Libby. You've been sleeping for hours. I think you should have something to eat, sweetheart.'

'I'm not hungry.' My voice is serrated and as dry as dust.

'I understand, but couldn't you just try some chicken soup at least?' *Chicken* soup? My mother must be desperate for me to eat. 'Please would you just try some?' She almost looks frightened.

I don't say anything and slowly lift myself up on the pillows. My limbs are cold and heavy; it was like raising the *Titanic*. Like that ship, I feel broken in two. Mum reappears holding a tray steaming with a chicken soup smell. It's only when she lays the tray down in front of me that I notice the small beige box nestling against the soup bowl for comfort and warmth.

Mum is watching me closely. 'I know it probably won't matter to you right now,' she begins quietly, 'but today is your birthday, Libby.'

My fingers find their way to the box and gently rub its neat edges. Yes, she's right, today is my birthday: I have been alive for fourteen years. So how come I feel so dead inside? Mum is trying to smile a gentle sort of smile but her mouth is quivering nervously. I return the box to the tray and rest the stern of my head back down amongst the pillows. She's right again – the day doesn't matter to me.

Mum swallows and nods. 'Have some soup at least.'

'I need to go to the bathroom first.' I'm looking at her expectantly; she'll have to move her face away from mine. It's all I can think of – I really just want to be alone.

'Yes, of course.' She jumps up and reaches out her hand for mine but I keep my head and hands down and focus my strength on swimming through the bedclothes.

The air is cold and heavy on my skin; it's going to take a miracle to raise this *Titanic*.

I really couldn't care less about bathing or brushing my teeth or being hygienic in even the vaguest sort of way, but the bathroom is just about the only place where I know I'm guaranteed some privacy. But it's not quite as much privacy as I'd like or need; every now and again I hear my mum's footsteps pacing outside the bathroom door. Sometimes they disappear entirely only to return a short while later, other times I can hear a brief pause in their pat-pat pacing. That's when I imagine her standing there with an ear pressed against the wood grain of the bathroom door separating us. That's just the sort of thing Mum would do. If I weren't so miserable I might even appreciate her concern.

But I lie in the bath for almost an hour – until the water is cool, with my big toes plugging each one of the taps to stop the plip-plop plip-plop sound of dripping water sending me even crazier. That's what the Chinese used to do to prisoners of war...drip water on their heads for hours on end. Chinese water torture can make a person crazy. I then brush each one of my teeth. Not once but twice. My reflection mirrors me perfectly as I run my tongue across my mouth's shiny enamelled smoothness. I always said that Sam had a smile with teeth just skew enough to be interesting. I wonder where that smile is now. Could it really have disappeared forever? I shake my head to dislodge the tears steaming up my eyeballs and use a towel to roughly swipe the liberated wetness from my cheeks.

There are voices coming from the living room but it's only when I exit the bathroom, all scrubbed up and shiny new, that I realise we have a visitor. It's Gloria, Sam's mum, talking to Mum. They haven't seen me yet. Gloria looks terrible. Her skin is also shiny, but that's because her face is swollen and red. The grey tracksuit she's wearing is creased and wilted and there's an elastic band making a half-hearted attempt at pulling her unwashed hair into some sort of order. She's been living on tears, wondering where Sam is too. Mum's fluffy white towelling dressing gown is wrapped around me tightly but I'm still cold. My feet are bare and my toenails are pink. I painted them in Manchester especially. I'm clean and painted. I suddenly feel sick with guilt and quickly make a move to slip from the room unnoticed.

'Libby!' That wasn't Mum so it must be Gloria's voice. I feel even sicker. *Why didn't I leave well enough alone – I wish I was still musty and dishevelled and dressed in crumpled, limp clothing too!*

I turn around slowly – any slower and my movements would be invisible. I wish I *were* invisible. 'Um...hello.'

Gloria's face is confused and hopeful and desolate all at once. Something tells me that she's been waiting patiently for some time to speak with me. Instinct also says that this can't be good. Her eyes are enormous while her gaze rifles through mine. She's expecting to find some answers today – anything to help see her through the next twenty-four hours. She needs a fix of faith and I'm her one great hope.

'How are you, Libby?' she finally croaks. My guess is that she knows I'm physically fine (there it is again – that hammer of guilt), so perhaps it's an update on my mental state she's after? Or maybe she's just being nice. After all, she's waited this long to find out first-hand about Sam's disappearance, so what are a few more seconds really?

Sorrow surges up my throat like fire; my chest is starting to burn again. 'I'm sorry, Gloria,' is all I can say before the tears get in the way. If I say anything more I'll drown in my words for sure.

Suddenly Gloria is right before me. She puts her arms around me and after a moment I weave mine through hers. As we stand there hugging, sobbing our silent sobs, I can't help but wonder at how small and frail she feels – like fragile bird bones in my hands. I also think about how many times Sam must have stood in this position, with his own arms clutching this person he loved so much. The thought makes me feel strangely closer to my missing friend. What I'd give to have him here with us right now. I'd give anything, absolutely anything. I gulp resolutely. If only we hadn't visited the beach that day. If only we hadn't taken a walk along the groyne. If only we hadn't kissed; we'd have been watching the ocean instead. If only we could rewind back to that glorious moment at Brighton's train station when Mum, Sam and me were so in love with life and each other. My mind is sick and infested with a thousand *if onlys*.

The flat of Gloria's hand is rubbing circles between my shoulder blades. 'Shhh now. Shhh. It wasn't your fault.'

Her voice is soft but her lips are near my ear so I catch every word. *It wasn't my fault.* I know Mum said that too, but how could I be sure? Mums say things to make you feel better.

'But if only…' I don't finish the sentence because I'm not sure how to. Instead I remain quiet and absorb the heat emanating from Gloria's rubbing. And after a while I even start to feel a little better. It's Gloria who finally breaks the moment. She pulls from me suddenly, levelling her head with mine and pinning me down firmly with her swollen red gaze.

'Now,' she begins with a heavy sigh that seems to come from somewhere deep inside her, 'you need to tell me everything, Liberty.'

Only my father calls me Liberty, and he's always annoyed with me. There's movement behind Gloria. Mum is shuffling from one foot to the other, looking uncomfortable...almost ready to pounce. Now I understand. Gloria has been through Mum first; she's assured Mum that talking is the best thing – for both our sakes. I can tell that Mum is no longer convinced.

I'm still staring blankly at Gloria; I'm not really sure what did actually happen.

'Libby, why don't you go and put some warm clothes on first,' Mum suddenly intercedes. 'Gloria, let's you and I make some tea. Then we'll all go and sit by the fire.' That's my mum – a shepherd of lost souls. With her at my side perhaps I can talk. Maybe together we really can work out where Sam has gone. Perhaps then we'll know how to find him again.

Mum finally agreed to help me make and distribute A4-size photocopied posters featuring a photo of Sam and the words:

<u>MISSING</u>

Sam Pejic is 15 years old, 5 ft 8 with wavy
dark hair. Distinguishing features: 1 eye dark,
the other a pale blue. He was last seen
wearing jeans, a green shirt and khaki jacket.
HAVE YOU SEEN THIS PERSON?

The poster also provides the phone number of the local police station as well as Mum's home number. Telephones aren't very New Age at all so it's a good thing I'm the reason she has one.

The photograph of Sam is black and white but there's no mistaking his lovely face and bold, striking smile. He is unforgettable. I remember the day I took this photograph – it was the morning of the End War Now protest march. We'd spent hours and hours making banners with slogans like GIVE PEACE A CHANCE. That was the morning the general secretary of the Vegetarian Society approached us to ask if we wouldn't mind making one or two posters with the words GIVE PEAS A CHANCE. And he was serious too. I remember that Sam and I laughed and laughed until our stomach muscles seized up. But that was only after the general secretary had disappeared; Sam would never have laughed at anyone. My talking thoughts have turned to the past tense, I suddenly realise. *How can I even think about giving up on him that easily?*

Right now Sam's face is smiling back at me like he doesn't have a care in the world. What I'd give to rewind back to that precise moment in time – I'd happily relive it for the rest of my life. Just like in that movie with Bill Murray – *Groundhog Day* – I'd live the same day over and over and over again until I died a wrinkled and monotonous but very happy OAP. Yes, that would suit me just fine.

Mum wasn't crazy about my Missing posters idea. She thought we'd be better off leaving it to the police, but I said I had to do something. It was the posters or my own private search party. I could tell that there were serious things Mum wanted to say to me but she finally gave in with a small sad sigh and agreed to the Missing posters instead. She even helped me make them. Now we're handing them out to the various shops and post offices along Brighton's cold Atlantic coast. The stack of posters in my hands has already reduced by half and I feel slightly more optimistic already. At least we're doing something. And if I'm busy then I won't have to think about Sam's smile and where it's disappeared to.

Right now I'm standing in the pedestrian square of the high street waiting for Mum, who has disappeared into the doorway of a small sandwich shop for two take-away cups of tea. It feels eerie to be out and about amongst the twinkling trees and cheery folk trailing tinsel and humming carols. I'm a ghost wandering through the crowds of festive and frantic Christmas consumers armed with lists and purpose. Their energetic strides and intermittent shopping smiles make them appear so vibrant and alive. Suddenly someone jostles me sideways and snorts; this is not a good place to be standing still.

There's a half-moon of men dressed in black clothing standing just a few metres to my right and they've begun singing in unison. A few curious pedestrians and pecking pigeons linger to listen and before long there's a small group gathered around the black-clad carollers. This immediately seems like a good space to loiter unnoticed so I amble over and join the onlookers in their business of looking. The men are neat and shiny and giving the carols all they've got with carefully rounded O lips and smoothly gyrating hips. Sitting on the pavement beside an open box wrapped in red and gold Christmas gift wrap is a sign: BRIGHTON'S GAY CHRISTMAS CHOIR. The fact that they're singing *I Saw Daddy Kissing Santa Claus* should have been my first clue.

A few appreciative audience members toss spare coins into the red and gold box on the pavement and the singers wink coyly in unison every single time to say thank you. My guess is they've been rehearsing this. I pat my own empty pockets and wonder what's taking Mum so long. The choir, now entirely warmed up, are gearing toward a vibrant, upbeat tempo and have just begun belting out a show tune I only recognise for the words 'Hey big spender!' There's another Christmas favourite then, the thoughts grumble. Still, everyone around me appears to be enjoying the show. I watch them all smiling and bouncing their shoulders to the music. Some have linked arms for warmth or just to be close. Everyone looks so happy. That's the thing about Christmas, it's a bit like recovering from a bad relationship – you tend to forget the bad times too quickly. They can cancel Christmas for all I care. I sniff the cold air and shuffle away from the crooners before they realise that I still haven't donated any coins to the red and gold box.

There's Mum – talking to an old lady wearing a floral coat. I notice she's balancing two Styrofoam cups while she nods in time with the old lady's fast-moving jaws. That's another thing about Christmas: all of a sudden everybody wants to talk to each other.

Suddenly there's a voice that stands out bolder and louder than all of the others here today. 'Sinners – repent!' it hollers. I snap my head this way and that, searching for the sound. 'Beware, the end is nigh!'

There's a man dressed in a long, coarse coat carrying an enormous wooden cross across his back. The cross is so large it stretches past the man's grey scraggly head by at least a metre, but that doesn't seem to be slowing him down. He's moving through the crowds, parting the Christmas outfits like the Red Sea and heading in my direction. I've seen street evangelists before – usually armed with a soapbox and a small bullhorn at the very most. I think I've finally found their leader.

'Only the love of God can save the sinners,' he declares with great authority, eyeballing the bystanders with contempt. We're obviously the sinners. So the man holds a one-way ticket to Crazyville, but he may also have a point. I'm intrigued but wary of moving any closer just in case I snag his attention, but that's OK because he's trudging my way anyway. That's when I notice that he's attached a single shopping trolley wheel to the bottom of the cross so that it rolls across the pavement. So Mr Crazy is also a cheat; as far as I know Jesus *carried* His cross. You really can't trust anyone to get it right anymore. Not even the crazies.

The man is now only yards away from me but for some reason my feet are soldered to the ground. I'm suddenly challenging Crazy to a game of chicken and I have no idea why. For a long moment it appears as if the man and his cross are going to mow me down. They finally stop moving just inches from me. Now the cross is hanging over my head too.

'You must beg for forgiveness, sinner,' Crazy blares at me with bulging eyeballs, 'or your end will be a fiery hell.'

I don't even pause to think. 'And who says this isn't hell?' I stare straight into the man's bloodshots. I'm suddenly inexplicably angry, angrier than I've ever been before. I'm so angry the world is scraping past me in a blur. My insides are boiling. My limbs are trembling uncontrollably. I can't keep my hands on the steering wheel any longer.

'You are one of the heathens!' Crazy shouts, sending spittle flying into the atmosphere. 'You are a filthy sinner.'

'I'm not the one who let him die!' I holler back. My protest surprises me. This is the first time I've admitted – to myself or to anyone, for that matter – that Sam may no longer be alive. But the revelation is a wound I can't help poking at. I need some answers. 'I thought God was supposed to watch over His children,' I continue challengingly and with some venom. Of course it never once occurs to me that I'm reasoning with a madman, which makes me just about as crazy as Crazy. But if Sam is dead, then I need someone to explain to me *why*. And Crazy just happened to be the first candidate to come along.

'You are a filthy sinner!' Crazy repeats, almost as if I hadn't said anything at all. 'And sinners must repent. Repent your sins now. Get on your knees and beg forgiveness from the Almighty. It's the only way!' His free hand – the one not clutching the wooden cross à la shopping trolley – jabs the air and waves to the heavens like a well-known friend.

He hasn't heard a thing I've said. He has a repertoire and this is it, to be repeated over and over as he travels the pavements, regardless of who he meets. Suddenly

I'm back at the steering wheel; *this is Mr Crazy I'm talking to!* I glance around, suddenly aware of the shoppers once more. Some are staring at me and my fellow loony, others are pretending they haven't noticed a thing. Then Mum appears, breathless and tealess. Her face is white with two patches of crimson planted on her cheeks, the consequence of her recent sprint over here.

'Are you OK?' she puffs. Her eyes are giving me the once over, looking for any visible signs of damage or distress.

'I'm fine.' I shrug dismissively, feeling just a teeny bit stupid.

'You are a filthy sinner!' Crazy suddenly shouts at my mother. This really is his entire playlist.

Mum swivels to her right and leans forward menacingly. 'Button it, whacko!' she growls back at him. It's not often you see her temper have a turn; usually she's all love and light. But pull her tail hard enough and you'd better be prepared for her bite. Crazy seems to know when he's beaten and eventually skulks off, the trolley wheel of his wooden cross squeaking with every rotation until finally the dishevelled man and the squeak have faded, leaving Mum and me alone in the crowd.

'So, what happened to our tea?' I blink innocently

and rock between the toes and heels of my trainers. My hands are shoved so deep inside my pockets I think my fingers may just bust through the seams.

'What was that about, Libby?'

Nobody seems to be giving me any answers today. 'What do you mean?'

'Is there anything you want to talk about, sweetheart?'

'Not really,' I reply casually and swallow hard. 'We should get going; these posters aren't going to deliver themselves.'

Mum stares at me for a few silent moments and then pulls my woollen hat further down to cover my ears. She smiles at me sadly. 'Come on, let's have a cup of tea and get warm first.' Maybe she understands that some things are so big they need more time.

We choose a coffee shop called Le French Café simply because it has an empty table. Le French Café in the blustery, seagull-poo-strewn seascape that is Brighton – what were they thinking? Mum has disappeared behind a door marked *To let* – the letter 'i' scratched out by some bored but bright-eyed kids, no doubt. I'm sitting and staring around at the café's do-it-yourself décor. The ceiling is concealed by a large suspended wooden trellis dangling with fake flowers and trailing plastic ivy. I think the false foliage was once upon a time the colour of cerise and green respectively, but years of dust and disregard have left it faded and murky. There are probably all sorts of things living up there too, some of which will no doubt fall and land in my hair without warning. I scratch my head subconsciously. The walls have been decorated with a mural of happy people drinking tea under umbrellas on a sunny sidewalk – painted by the owner's close relative, by the looks of it. I don't think a real artist would paint tea drinkers with door-jamb noses and eyes like frilly UFOs. There's a plastic orchid in a vase in the centre of our table and I begin fiddling with its silky petals while I wait for service or my mother, whichever comes first.

'Are you ready to order?'

There's a schoolgirl dressed in jeans and a boobage-hugging jumper standing over me. Somebody's made her wear one of the plastic orchids behind her ear, which is exposed by a high ponytail. That can't be easy. She's holding a notepad. She must be our waitress.

'Two teas please,' I reply. My fingers are dusty. Stupid table decoration.

'OK.' Her lips barely move; her face is actually bored stiff.

'Oh, excuse me…' I catch her before she about-turns.

'Uh huh.' That was a grunt, not a sign of interest.

I empty my face of all irritation and extract a Missing poster from my bag, holding it up for her to see clearly. 'Would you please put one of these up in your café window?' I keep my voice even; this is a mission for help, not pity.

The waitress glances from the poster to me to the poster to me. Her face has gone from vaguely interested back to being bored stiff. 'You'll have to ask the owner.' She then turns for the café counter.

'Excuse me.' That's me for the second time today. 'Would you please call the owner over for me?'

'She's not here.'

'When will she—'

'Tomorrow.'

'Well, could you take a poster and put it up once the owner—'

'You'll have to come back tomorrow.'

'Geez, what is your prob—'

But the waitress has gone. So much for her Christmas spirit then, my talking thoughts rant, suddenly glad for the dusty orchid behind her ear. And they call this the season of goodwill.

There's a small television on a perch on the wall above Le French Café's counter. The volume is low but I'm close enough to hear and see the midday news report taking up its screen, which shows the aftermath of a bomb explosion at a rally to honour some religious leader person somewhere. Now they're talking about banning religious gatherings altogether. Oh, except for those held at places of worship.

The waitress is staring in my direction. Her eyes are glazed but she could be looking at me. I'd like to slap her with that dusty orchid. Somebody's left their crumpled newspaper on the seat beside mine and I quickly pick it up and hide my face in its print. Non-Muslims in Nottingham are angry that graves in a council cemetery all face southeast to Mecca. British plots usually point east, as the Christian belief is that Christ will return from there. Both sides are now contemplating a protest march. Everybody hates everyone else. The world has gone mad.

'Hello, love.' My guess is that this is not the waitress speaking. I look up from the inky news page; Mum is back from the *To let* and sitting across from me. The waitress is obviously still spitting in my drink. 'Did you order a pot of tea?'

'Yup.' Just then a large woman wearing a shiny polyester Mrs Claus suit wedges herself into the table beside ours. Christmas really is in my face this year.

'Are you feeling OK?'

'Yup.'

'If you're tired we could finish putting up the rest of the posters tomorrow.'

'No, the sooner the better.'

'Well, I don't mind finishing the job if you need to rest.'

'No rest.' I shrug casually.

'What's the matter?'

My mood is quite obviously blacker than usual. My soul mate is officially missing and the world is full of people who hate those people who don't look and sound and believe exactly like them. That's what I'd like to say, but then I'd have to explain my feelings and I just don't have the energy inside me. 'Nothing,' I reply simply and stare out of the window.

Mum contemplates me for a while. 'Come on, Libby, let's forget about the tea and get you home,' she finally speaks, stretching her hand across the table for mine. And even though I'm way too old to be holding my mum's hand (especially out in public), I take it anyway. She looks too sad not to.

My father phoned again this morning and this time I didn't fake-sleep. We both said hi and then he said he knew about Sam and me and the wave, that he'd been worried sick and that he was very sad and very sorry.

You and me both, my talking thoughts croaked.

Thanks, I spoke out loud.

Was I coping, he wanted to know?

I exist from day to day, my talking thoughts murmured.

I'm fine, I spoke out loud.

That's good, he replied. And how was I physically?

I couldn't care less, my talking thoughts muttered.

I'm fine, I repeated out loud.

Perhaps I should catch the train to Brighton and spend a couple of days with you, he suggested.

Yes, that's just what I need, the thoughts snapped.

I'm fine – honest, I spoke out loud.

Was I managing to sleep alright, he wondered?

Awake I live the nightmare, asleep I dream the nightmare, the thoughts whispered.

Yup, I spoke out loud.

We then said goodbye and promised to speak again soon. Now I'm lying in Mum's bed with the covers pulled over my head. The world is quiet and dark and smells of my mum. I'm thinking about the Missing posters and trying to remember where and in what order we put each one up. I'm following a mental train of the posters for the third time this morning, and still I'm stuck at the chippie at the bottom of Pound Hill. I can't remember if we left the next poster at the launderette or the community centre. There's the telephone, ringing again. Mum must have left the portable handset on the hall table because the ring is very loud – it could be right here in the room with me. I don't stir, so there's only Mum to answer it.

'Oh, hello Lotus. Uh huh. Uh huh. They did. Uh huh. When? Oh right. Oh. Right. Yes. Bye.' Click.

Knock knock. I quickly shut my eyes and fake-sleep, even though I'm hidden by the bedcovers. Now there's the sound of the door opening.

'Libby?' The left side of the bed creaks and sinks with the weight of Mum's bottom. 'Libby, are you awake?' I keep my eyes squeezed so tightly shut it feels like my eyeballs are pressed up against my brain. 'That was Lotus on the phone,' she continues regardless. Perhaps she's onto my fake sleeping. 'I have to tell you something very important, Libby. Do you think you could sit up for a bit?' The air around me, once so soundless, sizzles in my ears. I shake my head wildly and remain huddled in the darkness that has me safely hidden. Maybe I'll stay here for ever.

'Do you want me to come back later?' The air has turned thick and sticky. I open my mouth and suck it up desperately. My chest is blazing. Mum seems to interpret my silence. 'Shall we talk like this then?' The seconds have lost their speed; I'm trapped in this moment. But Mum seems to understand. I feel her hand rest on what is my arm but to her must just look like a lump. Now she's rubbing, gently, backwards and forwards. 'Libby darling.' Backwards and forwards. 'Lotus is with Gloria.' Backwards and forwards. 'The police are there too.' Her voice wavers but her hand continues, backwards and forwards. 'They've found Sam's body.' Backwards and forwards. 'I'm so sorry, Libby.'

Thirty seconds ago I still had some hope that Sam was alive. But now that they have his dead body the world as I know it has been annihilated, like some nuclear holocaust – reduced to nothing in just thirty brief seconds. Now there's nothing left for me to cling onto. I am lost and really don't know where to turn. So for a while I don't say or do anything. I just sit there, empty. Inside me is a throbbing void, a vacuum of nothingness.

The first emotion I do begin to feel is bewilderment. It doesn't arrive all of a sudden, mind you; it rather seems to amble over the horizon towards me. I see it coming and as it grows bigger I quietly begin to wonder how Sam could possibly be gone from my life for ever. *None of this makes any sense.*

I don't recognise the next emotion right away, but it comes on swiftly. As it stampedes its way across the barren wilderness that is my cracked and dried up heart I identify it as a mixture of frustration and despair. *Sam dead? How can that be?*

And suddenly there's denial – without invitation or warning. *It can't be Sam's body. I don't believe it, there's been some mistake!*

Anger is a surprise guest that swats denial right out of the way. *It was only a stupid rogue wave! I survived it – so why couldn't Sam? He's bigger and stronger than me. He's a better swimmer too. He should have made it!*

Ah, now finally, here comes the rain. My eyes fill quickly and suddenly, the wetness spilling over and gushing down my cheeks like overflowing rivers after a flash flood. My shoulders quake and roll like thunder and the first cry to escape my lips is short and sharp, like a crack of lightning. My grief has become me, there is nothing else. My voice is a noisy feral wail that takes over and shakes me like a limp toy. Mum quickly untangles me from the bedcovers and pulls me into her arms. She rocks me gently while she tries her best not to cry too but I don't even notice. I can't see past my own sorrow. Every nerve and fibre and cell in my body is consumed by this outpouring of sadness that stems and seeps from my core. I will never see my lovely Sam again. I will never touch his hand or hear his voice or breathe his scent of Christmas spice. I will never again bask in the sunshine of his smile. There simply is no more Sam. And somehow we will all have to try to get used to that fact. The sobs grip my body and twist and squeeze me until there's nothing left of me that I recognise. I will never be the same Liberty Belle ever again.

Part Two
After

twelve
we only hurt ourselves

Sam's funeral service is being held this morning at a Christian Orthodox church. This is the religion he was born into, when he still lived with his birth family in Bosnia. Gloria made the decision out of respect for Sam and his family who were killed.

The church is on the edge of the chalk cliffs overlooking the ocean that Sam and I once worshipped, but it doesn't really matter where or what church this is. We're simply here today to say goodbye to Sam, the boy we loved so much. And that's what this day is about – our love for Sam. There are so many people here who each loved him in their own way, for their own special reasons. I always said he was irresistible. There are friends from the Artists' Quarter and the Peace Project. There are friends he juggled with and fished alongside and some who shared his classroom. There are friends with brown skin, tattooed skin and hairy skin. There are friends with wrinkles and others with mummy-fingers still clutched in their small chubby hands. There are friends with dyed-purple heads, others with dreadlocks and some with no hair at all. The world in all its colours, shapes and sizes has turned up today to celebrate the life and love of Samir Pejic.

A short while ago old Archie, who sold Sam's handmade mirrors from his stall at the Artists' Quarter, said his goodbye in the only way he knew how – by playing his bagpipes into the cold Atlantic wind while dressed in his full Scottish tartan regalia. I expected to cry but I've been staring with dry, blinking eyes at all these strangers around me instead. There's so much of Sam's life in which I never got to share. I feel so proud of him for touching so many lives – and so many different and diverse lives too. Sam never discriminated or put people into boxes with labels so that *he* could understand them better. He made the world a carefree and much brighter place. *So why are the prisons filled with bad people who will live to be seventy while someone so good had to die so young?* These are the thoughts rolling around and around in my head while I listen to Sam's friends stand up and one-by-one reminisce about my soul mate. The salted wind has eaten through my clothes and flesh and sunk its icy teeth into my bones but I don't care or even notice. I have other things on my mind.

A young boy with a warm complexion and a coarse brush of untidy black hair clambers to his feet. He's twisting his thin fingers and scanning the quiet crowd nervously. Finally he takes a deep breath and begins.

'When my brother and I travelled here with our family not many people accepted or liked us much – especially at our school.' He has an accent that sounds Irish but is a much faster and more garbled version than I'm used to hearing. I have to hold my breath and listen carefully to understand him. He begins tapping the shoulder of the young boy sitting beside him. They look like brothers.

'The kids called us tinkers, gypsies and pikies just to start fights.' He pauses for breath. 'And sometimes they got themselves a fight too,' he adds, puffing out his bony chest. 'But Sam was the guy who spoke out for us. And after a while they stopped giving us such a hard time. We won't forget him.' The boy tips his head and then sits down so quickly his descent is a blur.

Nothing else happens for a few moments.

'Libby darling, would you like to say something about Sam?' Mum squeezes my hand and musters up a very small smile made just for me. 'Do you feel up to it?'

But the decision is snatched away from me by the large, middle-aged man with a comb moustache. I recognise him from the market. He stands up and in a Polish accent announces that he'll always remember

Sam as the young man who took a moment to 'say a simple hello'. He doesn't add much more but I fill in the spaces. I've seen groups of teenagers nicking things from his stall before, jeering at him as they sprint away.

A few other people stand up to speak, some to say no more than how much they will miss Sam. Not all of the stories are elaborate; Sam was just a top human they will never forget. Finally someone at the very front of the church stands up. It's Gloria, and she looks pale and grief-stricken and grateful all at once. She has something monumental in common with these people here today: they all saw and loved what she saw and loved in her Sam. She's lost her family not once but twice, so today these people are her family. She turns slowly to the open faces.

'Thank you for coming here today,' she begins, 'and honouring a boy called Sam who touched and changed my life for ever. Not all of you will know this, but Sam, or Samir Pejic, came into my life as a war orphan. I adopted Sam after his family was killed in Bosnia's campaign of racial cleansing. He saw towns and villages destroyed, churches and mosques blown apart, and watched his family die in a civil war where people from different ethnic backgrounds could not exist peacefully side by side. He lost everything he loved because the

116

adults around him could not tolerate each others' differences. Sam vowed to live his life differently. And listening to each one of you speak here today, I now know that he never wavered from this ideal. You will never know the comfort your words have brought me today. My beautiful Sam's life may have been short but, oh boy, it was bright. He made every single moment count.' There are tears slipping down Gloria's face as she clenches her fist and nods her head resolutely.

I'm watching her closely; today has brought her a sense of peace I'm still trying to understand. If Sam was so good and made such a difference to our world, then why was he taken from us? He saw such tragedy and transformed it into triumph. He didn't deserve to die. He was owed a long and happy life. I just don't understand anything anymore.

People have begun leaving the church in small groups. Some are talking amongst themselves, others are moving quietly with thoughtful brows. Gloria has disappeared behind bodies focussed on hugging and stroking her while they smile and share a few more memories. The smiles – that's another thing I don't understand about today.

Mum still has my hand and leads me back out of the church into the cold wind. I turn to the horizon and bury my face in the blustery weather. The view from the chalk cliffs is breathtaking, literally. I have to breathe deeply to catch the scraps of wind pummelling my face. From this height the ocean looks flat and immense, a great body of wetness sloshing this way and that – depending on the mood of the moon. But this isn't really the ocean, not entirely, anyway. These opaque waves are just the tips of it. Beneath this choppy surface are endless fathoms of dark water and animals and plants growing from plains of sea beds so vast and wide we could never even begin to imagine it all. I'm just staring at its rippled outer skin. Sam called the ocean an ecosystem, I still remember. Mum is waiting patiently beside me, not saying anything – until now.

'Are you OK, Libby?'

I breathe deeply once more. 'I guess so.'

'What are you thinking about?'

'Nothing much. I just realised something, that's all.'

'And what's that?'

'That I don't believe in God anymore.' I don't think Mum will mind too much considering that she's spiritual rather than Bible-hugging religious, but her face suddenly squeezes into a frown.

'What do you mean?'

'What do you mean, "what do I mean"?' I'm trying

not to scoff at her but it's something to hide behind.

'You know what I mean. What do you mean?'

My head is starting to throb. 'I mean exactly that: I don't believe in God anymore.' I pause thoughtfully. 'If there was a God, do you really think He'd take somebody like Sam?'

At first Mum looks surprised. Now she's thinking of suitable replies.

'I don't believe that Jesus was born in a stable and died for our sins either,' I suddenly add, like it just occurred to me. I don't say anything further and watch her carefully picking through her words instead.

'Well, honey,' she finally begins, 'I don't know that it's quite that black and white—'

'Yeah, that's another thing, just who decided that Jesus was white.'

'That's not what I meant—'

But once again I don't let her finish. 'Did you know that more people have died because of religion than any other cause like war or famine or natural disasters?'

'Who said that?' Mum looks worried.

'You did,' I reply smugly. And she did, when I was younger – only she didn't actually say it directly to me. I overheard her enlightening my father after he insisted that I must, not-open-for-negotiation, be christened

Catholic. But Mum was resolute that I would choose my faith when I was old enough – or not choose, if that's what I wanted – *since more people have died because of religion than any other cause like war or famine or natural disasters.* Like the rest of the world, it seems that even my parents have argued over religion.

'Oh right,' is all Mum says. Now she recognises the statement as one of her own. 'Darling, you're going through an awful lot right now.'

'This isn't just about Sam.' I begin to strengthen my case. 'Look around you – religion has made the world crazy. Everybody hates everybody else and thinks their religion is the right one. Who is right and who is wrong – nobody has a clue. That just proves that there isn't a God.'

'Maybe those arguments stem from man's flaws and insecurities and have nothing to do with God,' Mum counters.

'Well, then isn't it time that God intervened and ended the argument once and for all?' But I'm losing the fight in me. I'm just so tired and sad and a thousand other emotions snowballed into one. 'This really isn't just about Sam...' my voice trails off miserably until there's nothing left of it.

This time Mum simply stares at me sadly for a very long time. 'Come on, let's get you home, love.'

I don't see or speak with Gloria for the next couple of days, but I think I hear Mum talking to her over the phone once or twice. And even though in my heart I know that Sam's death wasn't my fault, I still feel heavy with a burden of guilt I can't seem to shake from my shoulders. I'm almost sure that Gloria blames me, even though I have no evidence of this. I wonder if other people blame me too? I did contemplate standing up and speaking at Sam's funeral but the thoughts warned me that some of his friends might boo me out loud (or think badly about me at the very least). I am the reason Sam was standing on the groyne at that precise time on that particular day, after all. I had arrived from Manchester and he was giving *me* the tour. Had this been a normal day – a day not tinged with grief for the loss of my friend, I would firmly remind myself that the thoughts do tend to get carried away. I can be hard on myself. I am insecure; I need reassurance. But today is anything but normal and I simply can't find the strength to rein the thoughts in.

We return home from the church on the edge of the chalk cliffs and I keep myself busy by dismantling Mum's small shiny Christmas tree bit by bit. I have decided to boycott Christmas – especially now that I don't believe in God anymore. Christmas is, after all, a Christian holiday celebrating the birth of God's only son, Jesus Christ, even if this is a largely overlooked fact.

Mum doesn't mention the missing tree and tries to talk cheerily around the hole in the lounge instead. Maybe she's hoping that if she acts like everything's OK, eventually it will be. So she doesn't mention the tree, but she does try to get me to share my feelings. Usually I like talking to Mum, especially about my feelings. I don't get to do that much in Manchester. But these days I don't know how to talk about the things I have inside me. Sometimes I just feel empty, like the part of me that pulsed and sensed had drowned in the ocean with Sam. Or maybe I just don't *want* to feel better. Mum says that it won't be like this for ever. Grief is a process, she explained, and I must experience each stage so that I can heal and find some peace with the loss of my friend. I simply gave a nod in all the expected places. She makes it all sound so easy.

Now I'm back in Mum's plump bed staring at the

unframed and slightly curling photograph of Sam propped up against the bedside lamp. It's not the photo I used for the Missing posters. I felt so optimistic back then, convinced we were going to find him (a little battered and bruised perhaps, but alive and fixable for sure). No, this photo was taken by the fishing club for their members' board. He appears so vibrant, standing proudly – his back arched, holding his fishing rod and seaweed-green net-like trophies. Staring at the picture, for a moment I almost believe that if I reach out and touch his image I'll feel warm flesh and growing bones. *If I just believe hard enough.* When I was a young girl – so young I can't remember my precise age – I had a plastic baby doll called Tamara with soft blonde hair and the ability to wee when fed sufficient quantities of water from her special pink-teated bottle. For some forgotten reason I got it into my small head that if I looked after Tamara and gave her enough love and care she would eventually come alive. I absolutely believed that she would transform into a living, breathing baby. Until she just never came alive, that is. For a while I felt sad, then annoyed. Finally I boycotted her – just like Christmas – and left the stupid plastic doll to gather dust in a box somewhere dark. So much wasted loving, was all I could think about. Perhaps that was my grieving process for Tamara. That's the thing about photographs and baby dolls that wee – they can seem too real.

MY VICTORIAN STEREOGRAPH! Just moments before we mounted the groyne Sam presented me with a Victorian stereograph with three-dimensional postcards of the ocean! It was my birthday gift.

'MUUUUM?!'

The bedroom door flies open. 'Libby! What is it? Are you OK?' Mum's eyes are large and rolling.

'Where is it...my jacket...the brown one...I was wearing it that day...the day Sam and I were washed off the groyne?'

'Why, what's the matter?' Her face is pinched with confusion; her hands wide and open and jerking in time with her words.

'I NEED IT!' I'm crying again. Oh no no, not again.

'All right, calm down sweetheart. It's, uh...' She's trying to think about my brown jacket. Where could it be? She stares at the floor, concentrating hard, trying to remember. That day was a desperate blur. She raced to the hospital. I was already dressed in a hospital gown. The following day she took me home in the clean, dry clothes she'd brought in especially; the crumpled, now-dry jacket and jeans I had been wearing were in a plastic bag. The nurses were thoughtful like that. She took the clothes home and tossed the bag to the back of her own clothes cupboard: out of sight, out of mind – another problem for another time. Mum's brow collects in a frown. Now that she knows the location of the jacket she's suddenly not so sure if seeing those clothes again would do me much good. Not right now, she's thinking to herself. They have vivid memories woven through their salt-encrusted fibres.

'But you've got plenty of other jackets, Libby. In fact, I thought we might go and buy ourselves some new winter woollies. It might do us good to get out.'

'I. Must. Have. My. Brown. Jacket.' It's all I can manage; each word is a challenge and a victory against the fear squeezing the life out of me. I'll never forgive myself if the stereograph is gone for ever too. Mum really has no idea.

'All right, if that's what you want.' She sighs and finally turns to the cupboard. It only takes a moment for her to retrieve the bag from the darkness and place it quietly on the bed.

I make a grab for it, quickly tipping it upside down. My jacket! The brown material is stiff and crumpled – as choppy as the salty ocean it was pulled from. First pocket: empty. Wrong one, the thoughts pray. Second pocket: there's something inside. I yank the zipper open and extract the brown bag from the pocket pouch. I reach in for the stereograph and pull it gently from the clutches of the bag. My trembling fingers find the small brass clasp once more and release the wooden lid set with glass lens eyes. The postcards are still there. Now my movements are less hurried. I carefully run a fingertip across the first postcard. It feels slightly damp to the touch but the monochrome image of the boat with the billowing sails is still intact. It takes care and an extra helping of patience to extract the wad of postcards from the box and separate each one. Each postcard is wetter than the next. They didn't get much air trapped inside the wooden stereograph box. The fourth postcard, the one in the centre of the pile, is so wet it comes apart in my hands. *Stupid me!* I should leave them on the radiator to dry a little first. I'm so caught up in propping the various pieces of postcards against the heat of the radiator I don't notice Mum until my hands are empty.

I glance up to find her eyes wide. 'I don't want to talk about it,' I say and walk from the room.

fourteen
sights unseen

We're sitting in the lounge, our faces rippling with the choreography of the flames dancing in the fireplace. Mum is stringing colourful beads onto a thread and I'm staring at a hard-cover book about crop circles. Christmas is only a few days away but that's OK, because I've boycotted the day and Mum never really subscribed to the event anyway. I still can't help thinking about it though. I don't care about a Christmas lunch or the wrapped-up presents we're going to miss out on. It's the gaping hole of laughing friends and family that's going to be a challenge.

'Libby, do you remember your Great Aunt Flora?' Mum suddenly asks.

The name is a memory; the face an empty space. But I know that Mum speaks to her Aunt Flora often, or as often as you can speak with someone who lives all the way over in America. I shrug noncommittally.

'I don't expect you would remember her. It's been years since you last saw her; you can't have been more than three or four.'

Yeah, and? The thoughts don't really care.

'She's recently returned to England. She's settled in the Chesamere Valley, which is only a few hours' drive from here. And she's invited us to come and spend a few days with her.'

I still don't say anything.

'She's just gotten married – to a Welsh soil scientist, although they met in America. Can you believe that?'

A soil scientist? So he's like an expert on dirt. Ha ha.

'They now live on an organic farm. She's told me all about it. They have a goat pasture, an orchard and a veggie garden. They even have a pond and two ponies.'

That's super, if you're like six years old.

'So what do you think?'

'About what?' I still don't look up from the crop circles.

'About visiting Great Aunt Flora for a few days?'

I know what she means; I just need a diversion – time to think. 'Uh, I don't know.' That was obviously not enough time.

'Come on, it'll be fun.'

And a whole lot better than sticking around here for non-Christmas, is how the thoughts finish her sentence. 'I guess so.' I shrug for the second time.

Mum looks up wistfully from her threading. 'Flora has been like a second mum to me, bless her. Yes, I think it'll do us some good, Libby.'

But I don't want to hear about things that will do me good so I point my nose towards the book again. How come you don't get crop squares…or oblongs?

'We could leave this afternoon?'

'Fine by me.' Shrug. *What do I care?* But I pack a small travel bag and get myself ready as per Mum's instructions anyway. Right now it's just easier to let someone else do all the thinking.

Aurora's old clogged-up heater is not worth its on switch and I spend the journey with my arms crossed and my hands buried in my armpits. It's just as well I don't have BO. Mum's wearing a pair of home-knitted gloves that end at the knuckles but every now and again wedges a hand beneath her bottom for a bit of extra warmth. That's an extreme sport for a vegetarian bean-eater.

We don't say much and simply stare out at the world moving through glass – Mum through the windscreen and me alternating between the windscreen and the passenger window, which doesn't close all the way and whistles softly at the world. Like a constantly dripping tap, it's another form of torture to send me crazy.

I'm already wishing I'd refused to visit Great Aunt Flora's organic farm and soil scientist husband.

'What does that sign say?' Mum asks, peering over the steering wheel with eyes like almonds.

'Welcome to Chesamere Valley, land of nature and folks who nurture.' I can't believe I had to say that out loud. Even the thoughts are disgusted (and they're generally not fussy).

Mum looks at me and grins. 'Well, isn't that just lovely!'

Sure – a bit like a ballpoint up the nostril.

'I think we're almost there,' Mum continues. 'Yes, there it is!' Her mottled blue fingers are pointing to another sign that reads:

Pips & Stones Organic Farm
Happy Home of Frank & Flora
(and all things great & small)

Something tells me that the hours and minutes at Pips & Stones are going to pass like a mudslide.

Beyond the sign are two endless tyre tracks fringed with grass and trees and threadbare shrubbery. As Aurora squeaks and shudders her way along the dirt road I stare out at the surrounding scenery and contemplate my place in it. There's a small mucky pond with an island in its centre. We're talking clumps of mud held together by bushels of long grass trodden flat by a few bumbling ducks – you couldn't confuse it with the Bahamas. It's just as well we didn't pack our beach towels. Chugging further along the road I notice fields sprouting with various green-stalked things. Organic vegetables, no doubt. Meal times should be a real tastebud treat. Now there's what appears to be a paddock of sorts. I see drinking troughs and a pile of hay – for the animals to eat or sleep on, presumably. Ah, and there are the goats – funny, bearded creatures with kicking hooves and horns to make kebabs out of my calves. What fun this is going to be. The thoughts are less than impressed.

'I think that must be the house,' Mum mutters. She doesn't sound convinced.

The building up ahead is long and rectangular with soft, rounded corners, a front door with two large windows on either side and a sloping roof. Still, there's something inexplicably odd about it. Mum parks Aurora beneath a nearby tree and we both exit the icebox, desperate for a warm drink. At that very moment the front door opens and a tall woman with long grey wispy hair steps through its frame. She's dressed in baggy denims, boots and a check shirt with buttons.

'Iris – yoo hoo!' she hollers with a grin split like the Grand Canyon.

Mum jumps at the gesture but quickly recovers from her fright and yoo-hoo waves back. 'Come on, Libby – let me reintroduce you to your great-aunt.'

We haven't taken more than a few steps forward when G.A. Flora comes trundling down the stairs to meet us halfway. And the first thing she does is grip my head with her hands clasped over my ears and draw my face close to hers, like I'm severely short-sighted. 'Hello, Liberty Belle, I am Flora. It's been…what…about a decade?'

She has a very strange accent – British but with consonants that sound squished flat and vowels that seem to roll on forever.

'I, uh…' I'm bumbling – too busy watching her Americanised lips stretch around her English accent. I really have no clue how long it's been since I last saw her, but that's OK because she doesn't appear to be hanging around to check on my calculations anyway.

'And Iris!' G.A.F. gushes some more, releasing the ears. 'What happened to your hair? It's all gone. And it's as white as a goose!'

Yeah, that's how we describe it too. It seems the thoughts and Flora have something in common.

'Oh, right.' Mum almost looks embarrassed as she runs a hand over her hair.

'Did we do that after the divorce, dear?' Flora asks with a face that says: *it's OK, we all do crazy things sometimes.*

'Ah, I suppose we...uh, *I* did.' Now Mum really looks embarrassed. I don't think she'd ever put hair and the divorce together.

Suddenly Flora turns back to me. 'Can we talk about the divorce, Liberty? Are you OK with that?' Her face is creased with worry, like I may erupt and gush with hot lava-tears at any moment.

'Ya-ah, sure,' I blither. The question catches me unawares; no one has ever asked me that before.

'Well, I am so glad.' Flora smiles at me consolingly while gently patting the top of my head. 'Now come along you two, Frank is just popping a cork to meet you both.'

We don't reply and simply do as we're told. And it's as we're following this rather unusual branch of our family tree up the steps that a man suddenly appears at the front door. He's just as tall as Flora, but much thinner, with a long face made to look even longer by the pointed goatee beard he's modelling across the lower half of his face. His steel-grey hair is as wiry as a scouring pad and the fact that it's cut short at the sides and left much longer at the top seems to add to the overall length of his head.

'Are they finally here?' he sings and swivels his eyeballs to the left and right, pretending he can't see us.

Both Mum and I smile nervously and raise a hand like we're at a Star Trek convention. Greetings, mad soil scientist! The thoughts are almost enjoying this.

'You must be Frank,' says Mum.

'Ah, there they are!' he exclaims with all the enthusiasm he can muster (although this game is a lot more effective with five-year-olds). 'And right you are – Frank by name, cultivator by game. Welcome to our humble home, Iris and Liberty. Do come in.' He delivers scratchy kisses to our cheeks and then takes a deep step back, raking us into the house with grand, swooping arm gestures. We allow ourselves to be swept along and then loiter awkwardly in what appears to be the living area. I notice that two of the walls are lime-washed while the farthest wall is patterned with large flat silver stones. There's a glowing wood burner in the corner of the room hedged in by two floral sofas, a pair of small tables, a few rugs of colourful threads thrown haphazardly across the wooden floor and a large wicker basket brimming with chopped wood.

'The timber frame, cordwood, windows and doors of the house are all one hundred per cent recycled,' Frank the mad scientist explains without prompting, gazing around the room affectionately. We're obviously staring.

'Come on, let's get a brew on and I'll show you the kitchen.' Flora assumes leadership of the tour with twinkling eyes. She seems just as proud.

This looks like an odd little house to me but with the way these two are carrying on anybody would think they'd made the front cover of *Grand Designs* or something. But I only eyebrow-jiggle these thoughts at Mum as we traipse a trail through to the open-plan kitchen which, as it turns out, has a tree growing out of the floor beside the longest of the three kitchen counters. And why not. Both Mum and I are gawping. The tree is about five feet tall and a bit on the skinny side, with jagged, leafless branches. Still, it is winter – even if this is the great indoors.

'This was the perfect location for the house and we couldn't bear to chop it down.' Flora grins and stares at the tree like it's the child she couldn't bring herself to pack off to boarding school. The rest of the kitchen is just as I'm beginning to expect: lots of natural untreated wood (renewable forests, of course); a distinct lack of shiny gadgets with plugs (banish the electricity-guzzling thought); and various bowls and recycled pots brimming with fruit, herbs and vegetables (most of which still have mud clinging to their roots). But there is a cast-iron range cooker in view, which means that at least we won't have to tuck in to all the green stuff raw.

Looking past the tree, I notice an additional rectangular area packed with a large plain wooden table and six chairs. A dining room is good; it's civilised.

'Let me show you to your bedroom.' That's Flora again. No one else is saying much, although Mum is glowing. Her weirdo New Age-ness is obviously hereditary.

'You'll be sharing – I hope that's all right,' says the Great Aunt. We both nod, even though our hostess has already disappeared through another door and doesn't seem to be particularly bothered if we do mind. We follow her route.

The far wall of our bedroom is also patterned with more of the flat silver stones lining the living-room wall. The ceiling is a ribcage of exposed oiled timber beams. The double bed, or the closest thing to it in the room, is raised up on stilts made out of coarse wood with the bark still intact. There's a ladder reaching up to the bed and it's also made out of rough wood. It appears wider at the bottom than at the top and looks more homemade than sturdy. My guess is that Frank is the serial DIY-er. He looks the sort.

'Oh, this is just lovely!' Mum clucks. 'Thank you, Flora.' She smiles up at the older woman with genuine warmth.

This place is right up Mum's chakras, the thoughts note.

'Drop your bags and I'll show you to the bathroom. We don't want to get caught unawares, now, do we?' Flora smirks in my direction.

I have been working on my toilet training since we last met, I grimace silently. But Sam would have thought this all quite funny; he always saw the lighter side of our mad, earth-embracing mothers. Now I have a crazy great-aunt too. This makes me smile. Now I'm chuckling. Mum's looking at me nervously.

'It's always worthwhile knowing where the toilet is, huh Libby?' Mum's not sure why I'm laughing but she's hoping I'll remember my manners.

'Uh yes, definitely.' I wipe my eyes and take notice of the bathroom Flora seems so concerned with. There's a lovely corner bath, and instead of tiles, the walls are embedded with the round bottom-ends of glass bottles of every colour imaginable. The edges of the bath are crammed with bits of coral and shells and candles in curly holders, and directly over the bath – dangling above its very centre – is a large spiral windchime made out of cowrie shells.

'The toilet is behind the door,' Flora explains, 'although we try to limit its use to night-time only. There's a compost toilet outside for daylight trips. It has superb views.'

I make *ker-azy* eyes at Mum – welcome to the organic funny farm – but she pretends not to notice.

She sighs happily instead. 'You have a lovely home.' This is eco living – the real way to live. If Mum has talking thoughts, that's what they're saying.

Flora sighs happily. 'Yes, it was a real labour of love.' Now they're both smiling at me expectantly. I stare blankly ahead. Realising that she's not about to get a happy sigh from me too, Flora finally resumes her tour speech. 'This is one of the first straw-bale buildings in the county, I should mention. The house has a timber framework with straw-bale in-fill walls, which are sealed with a mixture of putty and sand, inside and out. The walls are then lime-washed. We've used only natural and sustainable building materials and methods and—'

'The tea is ready!' Frank calls out from the kitchen.

Flora looks disappointed; I'm so relieved I could kiss the man (but definitely won't). Right now I need a warm cup of tea, not a lecture on how to save the planet. And as for this house of straw, somebody has obviously not read about the Three Little Pigs.

Something hurts. I lift my right shoulder and extract the stereograph from the dent in my back. The ceiling is just a few feet above my head; I'm staring at dark wooden beams that run in the same direction as my horizontal body. It takes me a few slightly anxious moments before I remember where I am. Ah, the organic funny farm.

The other half of the bed in the sky is empty, or it would be – if I wasn't sprawled out like a starfish beneath the covers, which are, incidentally, covered in brown batik giraffes. The look is not IKEA. I wonder where Mum can be? I wish she were still here beside me, I'm a bit wary of encountering freaky Flora and the mad scientist on my own. Plus my bladder is full. And it's definitely daylight outside. I wonder if I'm expected to go in search of the outside compost loo? Just the name puts me off. I'm not sure how many kinds of compost there are, but I only know of the manure sort. This day does not look promising.

I slip the stereograph safely beneath my pillow and climb carefully down the roughly hewn ladder. There's only silence. The house of straw appears to be empty so I might as well chance the indoor toilet with its colourful wall of bottles. I close the bathroom door quietly behind me, just in case. The milky winter sun is streaming in through the window and ricocheting off the bottle ends, creating a kaleidoscope of rainbow hues that shimmer and twinkle like embedded jewels. I make a mental note to bath only when it's light outside, and soon after exit the bathroom on stealthy feet. But the air is still silent.

The heat of the range cooker intensifies as I approach the kitchen. The Scrabble board is still open on the coffee table. Aubergine lasagne and triple point scores – what a special time last night turned out to be. If I thought being in a new and different environment might help me work through my thoughts of Sam I was wrong. Everything still feels strange and cold to me; I'm so far away from everything I recognise as safe and familiar. I tried to get into last night's game of Scrabble but the word 'green' was my high point, earning me a score of six. Eventually I made my excuses and trundled off to our bedroom where I lay beneath the brown batik giraffes and gripped my stereograph tightly, rubbing its wood grain reassuringly with the pad of my thumb. Mum came in a short while later. She understood.

I blink the memories of Sam and the Scrabble board from my eyes and survey my surroundings. There's a folded note and a loaf of seed bread on the counter beside the tree that's growing out of the floor. Mum's hand has written my name on the note. I open it up and begin reading. There's tea in a pot on the range cooker. The bread is for breakfast, with honey. I glance around. There's a recycled, unlabelled glass jar of gooey gold standing beside the seed bread. Of course they don't do supermarket bees at Pips & Stones. I drop my gaze back to the note: Mum, it seems, is 'exploring the great outdoors' and helping Flora and Frank with their farm chores. I only need to come calling to find her, she writes. Farm chores? Yeah, as if.

But as it turns out I eventually do come calling because, after a breakfast of tea, seed bread and honey, there's not a lot to do in somebody else's gadgetless straw house situated in the great metropolis of Nowhereville. So I set off walking with the smell of fresh dung in my nostrils and the spring of fresh earth underfoot. The farm appears bigger than I think both Mum and I first realised and I'm really not sure where to begin my search. So I head in the direction of the goats, simply because they're the first to catch my eye.

I can only spot two of the cloven-hoofed creatures.

One is brown with horns and the other is black and white with large floppy ears. Both have bellies shaped like inflated rugby balls. Perhaps they ate all their mates. They both have goatee beards too – their claim to fame. Maybe Frank, as well as being a lover of all things soil-related, is a big fan of goats. He has, after all, grown his facial hair just like the domesticated mammals, so it's not unlikely. They do say that people eventually start to look like their pets. Last night Frank rolled down his sock and showed me his ankle decorated with a tattoo of an earthworm. Seems the earthworm is nature's way of aerating the soil, which is precisely why mechanical ploughs are bad, bad, bad. They slice the poor worms up like cheddar through a grater. He almost had tears in his eyes. Something tells me that Frank had a tough time of it at school.

I say goodbye to the goats and continue along the worn path. Winter has reduced every tree to a carcass and chilled the ground solid so that my shoes slip off rather than slide into the mud track. I actually feel a bit silly walking around the farm calling out my mum's name. It's so quiet here. There's a wind running through the lifeless grass but the green blades are still heavy with morning dew and not yet up for the game. I sniff at the air. It has a bouquet I don't recognise, although I think

I detect faint notes of warm farm animal and fertiliser. And all around me is still silent.

But not for long. 'Muuum!' I holler. Once again, nothing. Where is she?

Set back from the path and to my left is a terrace of what appears to be small animal shelters constructed out of raw breeze blocks and old wooden doors wilting at the hinges. The shelters don't look like they've been used for some time, or not for animals, anyway. Most are filled with an assortment of piled-high sacks, terracotta plant pots, rusted drums, some well-used gardening tools, a stack of faded plastic chairs and two tractor tyres.

Now that I've warmed up a little I'm almost starting to enjoy my walk. The ground ahead is beginning to dip, assuming the sloping gradient of a wide open valley. The world and its busyness seem to have dissolved into the background, leaving me feeling free and my head less cluttered with noise and confusion. Instead of slumping my shoulders, dropping my gaze and shrinking into the bustle, for once I feel like I can lift my chin, breathe deeply and engage with my surroundings. Today life isn't crowding me out. I'm no longer sure I want to find Mum just yet.

A short distance beyond the breeze blocks is another

construction, only this one stands approximately two metres high and is made entirely of wood with corrugated plastic sheeting on the roof. Moving forward in a semi-circle, I find what appears to be the front of the structure – facing the slope of the valley. It has two doors, both of which are closed and neither of which reaches the full height of the building. Each door probably measures just over a metre in length and is raised a foot or so from the floor. Someone has taken the time to fill old yoghurt pots with plants and attach them to the frame of the building. I'm imagining how pretty this must look in summer while my palm is poised flat against one of the doors, ready to push.

All of a sudden there's a man's voice. 'Is that you, Flora?' It's coming from inside, beyond the door. Now there's a scraping sound. A pointed old boot, a furry sock and a bit of leg have suddenly appeared beneath the gap in the door beside me. And there's an earthworm tattooed on the leg's exposed hairy ankle.

Frank?

The whiff in the air has intensified to an aroma that's definitely more fertiliser than warm animal. I think I may just have stumbled upon the famous compost loo. The thoughts are distraught. I'm instantly paralysed. I don't even breathe.

'If you've come for the *Organic Farmer's Weekly*, I'm not done yet.'

Oh, yuk! The pressure is starting to build in my head but I remain silent and still.

'Hee hee. We're not playing the naughty game again are we, Flora my filly?'

Eeugh, double yuk. I am the stupidest person in the world. I am a billion times stupider than the most stupid person in the entire universe. But I just let the thoughts rant and I don't speak out loud. Or breathe.

'Uh, who's there?' Frank is beginning to sound nervous.

I gingerly peel my palm from the door and take one slow, careful step backwards.

'Whoever you are, I can hear you!'

Another step.

'What do you want?'

I've got to breathe. Suddenly the earthworm disappears back beneath the door. Now there's the muffled and frantic sound of clothes fibres brushing, belt buckles buckling and whatever else – I don't stick around to find out. All I care about is making a U-turn and a mad scramble for cover. But I don't make it. Not even close. I hear the door of the compost loo bang open before I'm even halfway hidden.

'Oh, Liberty. It's you!'

I'm standing in a clearing – the nearest tree is still metres away from me. Not that it matters, I'd only look sillier trying to hide now. I turn very slowly.

'Uh, hi Frank.' I smile thinly. His copy of the *Organic Farmer's Weekly* is rolled up and poised in the air, mid swat. What was he expecting to meet, a giant fly?

'So sorry if I scared you, my dear. Ho ho. One never can be too careful.'

Yeah, mind where you point that rolled-up magazine, the thoughts grumble. We don't like to look embarrassed. And besides, Frank was the scared one.

'I'm looking for my mum,' I explain in a businesslike tone.

'Oh right.' He grins broadly. 'Well, come along and I'll take you directly to her.'

I don't even ask and simply fall in step with this strange man while I mumble a thank you.

'That was our compost loo,' he suddenly clarifies with a backwards thumb-jerk. He's still smiling proudly. The man has no shame. 'They really are marvellous inventions. You see, the problem is this: our planet is running out of water and so much of it is simply being flushed away. Here at Pips & Stones we call it the "rush to flush"! Ha ha. But what we must all

147

remember is that our waste – that is, the stuff our body can't or won't use – is a very valuable resource for the environment. It makes compost, which is a wonderful alternative to chemical fertiliser. And it really is something we can all use, so instead of *man*ure, we call it *humanure!*'

That's strange, we call it YUK! But Frank is oblivious to the thoughts.

'The heat generated by the aerobic decomposition of our waste,' he continues unfazed, 'is enough to evaporate the collected liquids – including urine. The generated heat also provides natural ventilation, keeping the toilet fixture at a slightly negative pressure, which eliminates smells. It's a wonderful, wonderful invention.'

'So where's my mum?' I quickly ask. I can't believe the man is still talking about poo.

'Ah, your mum,' he remembers, looking confused for just a moment. 'She's in the polytunnel with Flora. They're waiting for the IVOFs.'

He suddenly seems excited, or even more so than usual. I, on the other hand, very rarely seem to know what the man is talking about (which is probably just as well considering that the small bits I do understand seem to relate to his bodily functions).

He's now staring at me with his mad soil-scientist face and an expression that begs: aren't you even going to ask?

All around us is silence. I'm really not going to.

'IVOFs are International Volunteers on Organic Farms,' he bursts out, unable to contain himself any longer. 'We offer food, accommodation and invaluable experience on our organic farm in return for eight hours' work a day. They help us with everything – the goats, veg, orchards…sunrise to sunset – we're always on the go. And they come from all over the world.'

Yeah, that's generally what international means.

'We meet some very interesting people, too,' he stammers, looking slightly disappointed by my lack of interest.

Now I feel bad. Why do people do this to me – FORCE me to get involved in their lives! 'I bet you do,' I finally rally, attempting a weak smile. 'IVOFs, uh, tend to be the most interesting of all.' So I still have no idea what we're talking about. But the good news is I can see Mum up ahead, standing beside Flora and an enormous dome shape made out of plastic. I want to run into her arms, away from the crazy talk, but I continue at a steady pace with my head held high. Frank spies them too.

He waves when we're just a few metres away. 'Hiya, ladies.'

Mum spins in our direction and then quickly turns away again, dropping her head and bringing her hands to her face. Flora looks surprised but gives a slow, gentle wave back. Mum finally turns to face us again. I'm now standing directly in front of her red eyes and blotchy, salt-stained cheeks.

'Well, good morning, Liberty Belle,' my great-aunt greets me warmly, wrapping an arm around my shoulders. 'So how did we sleep?'

I wonder if that's a figure of speech or if she knows about the thoughts. 'I slept very well, thanks,' I reply. I like to maintain an outward image of sanity.

'That's good, sweetheart,' Mum says, her smile drooping sadly at the corners. 'Did you have something to eat?'

I nod but don't speak my reply. I'm too busy staring at her. Why was she crying? Is she also still sad about Sam?

'Liberty discovered our compost loo…with me in it. Ho ho!' says Frank.

More poo talk. 'You can call me Libby,' I instruct both Frank and Flora. All this Liberty business reminds me of my father and Manchester. And I'm eager to distract their attention away from the tale about the compost loo before Frank even begins it.

'Libby it is.' Flora smiles at me fondly and taps a hand on my head. I hate people touching my head, but I remain ramrod straight and silent because I don't want to appear rude. 'I remember that when you were a little girl your hair was short and as curly as a pig's tail.' Now Flora is smiling at Frank. 'She really was a cutie.'

So apparently we were pig-headed even back then, the thoughts joke. This doesn't happen often. Everyone is staring at me and my head.

'So what are you two up to?' I ask Mum and Flora and purposefully turn from Frank. The man needs no encouragement.

'We were just chatting and catching up,' Flora replies and reaches for my head once again. This time I bob-and-weave and bend to fake-scratch my knee.

'We're off to get some bedding out of storage,' Mum reveals. 'Fancy giving us a hand?'

My face is showing a negative.

'Or you could hang around here and help Frank with a few things?'

'You can read my *Organic Farmer's Weekly*, if you like?' Frank adds to the pot, offering me the magazine on an extended arm.

Eeugh. *Organic Farmer's Stinky*, more like. 'I'll come

with you, Mum,' I announce, taking a single step away from the offensive reading material. I'm going to have to keep a close eye on this bunch. Since arriving at Pips & Stones my mum and her New Age Brighton cronies suddenly seem extremely normal.

Mum, Flora and I are standing inside a narrow, lean-to-style addition to the rear of the straw house. This is 'storage', as my great-aunt calls it – a wall clad in deep shelving packed with all sorts of things from plant food and seeds to edible supplies, bottles of golden liquid (that look suspiciously homebrewed), some books – recipe and gardening mostly – and a few plug-free appliances (household or farming related, I'm not sure which). There's even a stack of board games. And folded along the very bottom shelf is an assortment of sheets, pillows and blankets – bedding for the IVOFs who may (if we take any longer) find themselves being greeted by Frank and his (now-very-organic!) *Farmer's Weekly*. IVOFs – I shake my head. I'm almost expecting a flying saucer with flashing lights to land in the goat paddock.

'Libby?'

I'm so caught up in notions of shelves and flying saucers I haven't been listening. So if that was a question, I have no idea what the answer is. Both women are looking at me expectantly though.

153

'Do you mind if the volunteers stay in the house with us?' Flora says, repeating what I think might have been the original question. 'They usually stay in the larger bedroom – the one with the double set of bunks.'

'In the straw house?' What, like a bunch of aliens – or, uh, strangers? Then again, nobody is stranger than Frank.

'Flora and Frank do know them,' Mum adds, smiling gently. 'This is the third year this particular group of volunteers will be staying at Pips & Stones.'

'Just how many are there?' I ask. They must be quite small if an entire spaceship-full is going to fit into the double bunks.

'Only four,' Flora pauses counting the bedding to reply. Three ladies and one fella.' Her Americanised tongue flips the last word up in the air like a pancake.

'Oh right. Well, why would I mind?'

'I just don't want you to feel uncomfortable.' Flora reaches for my head and then thinks better of it.

We passed uncomfortable a long time ago, the thoughts chirrup, reminiscing back to Frank and the compost loo.

Flora hoists a stack of sheets and blankets off the shelf and plops them into Mum's waiting arms. 'You can just leave them on the bed, thanks, Iris.'

Mum disappears to do Flora's bidding while I stand

there staring at my great-aunt's back while she scrounges around, searching for something.

'How are you holding up, Libby?' she suddenly asks, still facing forward.

So that was an unexpected question. 'I...uh, fine,' I stammer.

Flora turns to face me. 'Your mum told me about Sam. I hope you won't mind, but I wanted you to know how sorry I am.'

I'm feeling uneasy and searching for a window to stare out of. Of course I realise that Flora means well but I'm protective of my grief. The loss of Sam still seems very personal and private to me; I really don't think I'm ready for casual mentions from somebody (blood relation or not) who never even knew Sam. Mum should have kept quiet, because if you didn't know Sam then you'll never understand. And there's such a fine line between sympathy and pity. But it's too late now.

'Thanks, Flora,' I reply politely. She looks like she's contemplating hugging me so I quickly change the subject. 'Is there anything else you'd like carried over to the bunk beds?'

My great-aunt watches me with her intense pale eyes for a moment. 'You can take these, thanks, Libby,' she finally says and then hands me a stack of soft, knitted blankets. 'The volunteers should be here soon. We'll off-load these in the bedroom and hopefully make it back outside before they arrive. I do love to be there to greet them.' She grins, swiping a few rampant grey wisps of tickly hair from her face with her forearm. But my face doesn't have a grin. I'm not feeling the IVOF joy.

But Flora gets her wish, sort of. After depositing the bedding in the room with the double bunks Mum, Flora and I make it halfway down the drive, heading in the direction of the Pips & Stones signpost, when Frank and four new faces wearing backpacks come trundling up the road toward us. The first thing I notice is that the male New Face is clutching Frank's magazine.

'HIYA!' That's Flora. And she's waving like a banshee at Halloween.

All four New Faces wave back and grin like they're finally home. It only takes us a few short paces before we're all level and facing one another. Everyone except for Flora, that is, who is hugging each one of the New Faces passionately. Mum and I stand by quietly; we both seem to be using this moment to examine the arrivals closely.

There's a girl with bobbed light brown hair wearing combat trousers and well-worn boots. There's another girl with oil-black skin and an untamed afro that looks like a halo. This girl is wearing jeans and a dark blue jacket. Third in line is a lanky man with long dirty-blond hair and matching bristles on his New Face. His clothes are all co-ordinated in faded khaki. And finally, there's a tall girl with a strong body and black hair braided into two long plaited ropes that almost reach the scarf tied around her slim waist. I stare at *this* New Face the longest. She is extraordinary. Her skin is as smooth and warm as a chestnut. Her forehead is high and her nose long and sloping, hedged in by two beautifully arched cheekbones that make her face seem heart-shaped. I travel up to her eyes and discover that she's looking my way. They are so dark it's not easy to follow her gaze, but I can feel its weight resting on me. She's also watching me closely. Her face is neither friendly nor judgemental; she's simply looking.

Flora has finished hugging and is now standing between the New Faces and Mum and me, glancing excitedly between us. She has her finger raised in the air. She's pointing at Mum first.

'Iris and Liberty, this is Wil de Jong, Ky'a Wilson, Drew Lewis and Shawn Redd. Wil, Ky'a, Drew and Shawn, meet Iris and Liberty Belle – my niece and her daughter.' Flora is still glancing excitedly from one to the other, only now she's silent and waiting with a look that says we're all her special children and she's simply desperate for us to love one another just as much as she loves each one of us.

Suddenly everybody moves as one.

'Oh hello.'

'Hi there.'

'So nice to meet you.'

'How are you?'

'Hiya.'

Everyone except for Shawn Redd and me, that is. We remain unmoving, still staring and working each other out. Her face looks young and fresh – she's probably about twenty-something years old, just like the rest of the New Faces. But her eyes...to me they seem to be very old (not as in misty and crinkled, but in an all-knowing-all-seeing sort of way). There's a peaceful energy about her, vibrating from her being in long, slow cool waves. The effect is hypnotic. I couldn't even begin to guess what she's thinking about me. But finally there's movement. She dips her head slowly, first at me and then at Mum.

'I'm Shawn Two-Rivers Redd, nice to meet you.'

'Hello there.' Mum smiles and extends her hand. Shawn Redd touches it and then looks at me.

But I'm still thinking about the name Two-Rivers. My

guess is she's Native American. Looking at her, if it wasn't obvious before then it certainly is now. 'You can call me Libby,' I suddenly offer.

Shawn Two-Rivers dips her head and smiles softly. But she doesn't say anything more.

'Shawn is from North America,' Flora confirms in her tour-guide voice. 'And Drew is from New Zealand, Ky'a is Jamaican and Wil is from Rotterdam in Holland.'

'Hi,' I repeat once more, stretching the word across the three remaining volunteers. They all smile and greet me in return, except for Drew, who steps forward to shake my hand. He's going to use his *Organic Farmer's Weekly* hand too. I don't have time to dodge the approaching limb with a fake-scratch or a garbled excuse and before I know it, my right hand is being gripped by *that* hand. Eeugh. Suddenly I'm back at the compost loo with Frank. But Drew seems unaware of my torment and soon slips blissfully back into place in the line-up of New Faces. Shawn Redd is still watching me with one of her eyebrows raised ever so slightly.

But Flora's loud voice ends the quiet moment. 'Come on you lot, let's get you inside and warmed up with a cuppa!'

This is obviously a unanimously good idea because the volunteers waste no time falling in step with Flora and jostle to bring her up-to-date with their most recent exploits. There's excited talk of a bio-dynamic garden in Bulgaria, a mention of hot summer days spent on an organic mustard farm in Nepal, and an update on a drip irrigation system established in Mexico. And it's taken days of boat trips and train journeys to weave their way back to England and Pips & Stones Organic Farm. Shawn Redd has the least to say, but she smiles a lot and shows her interest by bending slightly forward at the waist while the others share their stories. I keep close to Mum and don't mumble a word. I don't really have anything to say. Even the thoughts are quiet and mulling over the volunteers' arrival. They may be from different parts of the world but their collective and very obvious passion for the planet they inhabit seems to unite them. They really are citizens of the world.

We all clamber inside the straw house and Flora sets to work brewing pots of tea while the volunteers scurry between their bedroom and the living area. Everyone is talking and Mum joins in the din by inserting laughs and short comments whenever there's a lull. I'm still standing there, hands in pockets, and not doing much else.

'Frank, collect two more fold-up chairs from storage, won't you, darling. Come on, we'll have tea and cake at the table,' Flora suggests, easing a large, lopsided cake from a tin. She catches me watching. 'Homemade,' she grins. 'And from home-grown carrots too.'

I don't know what else to do but smile a reply. If Sam were here he'd be right in there with the rest of them, nattering away like they were all old friends. He was just that sort of person. Of course Sam is still on my mind, this hasn't changed. Lately I find that I'm able to think quiet, everyday thoughts about him and incorporate his memory into my day-to-day living. He's now the invisible friend I keep close for comfort. Mum says that grief is a process. Lately my own grief is less angry and instead of crying constantly, I seem to sit quietly – adjusting to the emptiness. Everything takes some getting used to, they say.

Frank has returned with two fold-up canvas chairs and he squeezes them in between the wooden chairs surrounding the dining table while discussing the merits of worm bins with Drew. Flora is busily dishing out mugs of vaporous tea to K'ya, who is carrying them to the table and describing the rain-catchment system she's devised. Mum and Wil were admiring the teetering cake. Now they're focussed on Shawn Redd's wrist.

'Libby, come and take a look at this,' Mum calls out to me and points to the outstretched arm attached to

Shawn, who is watching me quietly once more. I do as I'm told and shuffle over to the wrist in question. We're all staring, it seems, at an inch-wide silver bracelet engraved with a repeated abstract tribal figure that appears to be blowing into something.

'Isn't it lovely?' Mum smiles in my direction.

'It's a Hopi Kokopelli bracelet,' Shawn Redd offers. She's still gazing at her wrist. She moves her head slightly. Her deep black eyes are once again watching me from under heavy lids. 'Kokopelli is the whimsical, mystical three-thousand-year-old flute player,' she says in what I swear could be a sinister whisper. 'He is a source of music and dance, spreading joy to those around him.'

'Ah, fascinating.' That's my nosy mother again. 'And what does Hopi mean?'

'The Hopi are Native Americans living in North America.'

'Oh right.' Mum looks like she's gearing up for another question but Shawn gets in there first.

'I am a Hopi.'

'Come along, everyone take a seat,' Flora suddenly orders. 'There's milk and sugar on the table. Grab a mug and dress it yourself. Frank darling, you cut the cake.' Everyone obeys and Frank takes his place at the head of the table, knife proudly in hand like he's about to carve a Christmas turkey. All the seats are quickly claimed except for one: I am, it seems, destined to sit between my mum and that slightly scary Shawn Two-Rivers Redd. But I soon have a plump slice of cake and a mug of steamy tea in front of me and I quickly put my energies into that.

'Wil,' Frank begins, looking directly at the girl wearing combat trousers, 'what have you been working on at Greenpeace since we last saw you?'

Everyone is instantly quiet and staring expectantly at Wil, who has a mouth crammed with home-grown carrot cake. She points to it while she chews. 'Climate change,' she splutters, finally swallowing. 'I've been trying to educate people about climate change – trying to get them to understand,' she explains in her guttural Dutch accent. 'The earth is warming up. And if we continue at our current rate, a continued temperature rise of two degrees Celsius could cause more floods, storms and droughts with one in four species possibly becoming extinct. This is the urgent message we're trying to get out there. But so many people don't want to listen.' Her eyes spark as she speaks passionately.

'Why don't they want to listen?' I suddenly ask out loud without consciously setting out to do so. I was expecting that question to remain a talking thought.

Now everyone is looking at me, including Shawn Redd. I can feel her heat.

But Wil is smiling at me gratefully – like she only wishes more people would take the time to ask. 'We need to change from a world powered by nuclear and fossil fuels to one that runs on renewable energy. Generating electricity uses so much energy, mostly heat produced in coal, gas and nuclear plants. This contributes to a warming world. But people don't like change…'

K'ya is fidgeting in her seat – she can't remain silent any longer. 'People can't see the big picture,' she adds with great gusto. 'People don't seem to understand that our planet is living and it needs looking after…which is surprising to me considering that we still haven't stumbled upon another planet suitable for us to live on once we've destroyed this one!'

I'm listening and watching carefully. In a strange way, K'ya reminds me of Sam. He was also very aware of the world around him and his place in it. The thoughts rewind back to that fateful day on the groyne. Sam was intrigued by even the smallest sea creatures and he talked about the ocean as an ecosystem. I think he'd be supremely pleased that I'm spending time and taking a moment to listen and learn from people like K'ya and Wil. He'd be quite proud of me I'm sure.

seventeen
rising steam

Today is a big day at Pips & Stones: Frank and Flora have bought two cows, and they're arriving this very morning. Everyone is abuzz. You'd think they were rock-star cows, the thoughts grumble. I haven't had my morning cuppa yet and all this bustle and excitement is too much for me. And I should really still be asleep. Thanks to the exuberant New-Face-IVOFs my cosy slumber came to an abrupt end at 5:53 this morning. They're a noisy lot. Worse yet, my finely tuned instincts tell me that this early-to-rise business is not a once-off. I'm sitting stooped over the dining table with my nose practically touching its top. I haven't brushed my hair and I have no idea what I'm wearing. But as long as it's not my pyjamas, I don't think I really care. Honestly, it's still not even quite light out.

'Here you go, darling.' Mum places a mug of steamy tea beside my wilted head and immediately returns to the bedlam that is the open-plan kitchen. Flora is toasting bread, K'ya is buttering the toasted slices, and Drew is frying tomatoes. Or at least I think that's what he's doing.

His long hair is still untied and like me, he's also sagging and drooped at the waist. Another non-morning person, I'm relieved to note. Shawn Redd, Wil and Frank are already outside doing who-knows-what. Crazy lot. I yawn so wide my jaw practically comes unhinged.

'Whoa, Mrs Hippopotamus! You'll swallow us all up if you're not careful.'

Great, Freaky Frank is back. Just be grateful that I've brushed the teeth already, the thoughts growl in his direction. And we'll let the Mrs Hippopotamus comment slide. Never let it be said that the thoughts aren't charitable.

'It smells great,' Wil says, removing her woollen gloves and rubbing her hands in anticipation.

K'ya turns from the cooker. 'These tomatoes look about ready.' Everyone scurries for a plate and toast. The unexpected movement startles Drew, who emits a small, sharp yelp.

'Uh yeah, like uh, help yourself, hey.' He bobs his head for confirmation. He's just remembered where he is.

Mum sits down beside me and slides a plate of fried tomato-topped toast beneath my nose. I'm soon surrounded by bodies all eating like it's a race and it's not long before they're dabbing at their chins over empty plates. I'm finding this excess of energy very unnatural. K'ya notices my droopy mood and leans over to squeeze my shoulder and offer up a grin that says 'cheer up, the day will get better'. I attempt to smile back at her and almost succeed.

'Right!' Flora smacks her lips and hands together. 'Are we all ready for a cow or two?'

A cow? I can barely finish this toast. Ah right, I see what she means. Even the thoughts are still half asleep. But everyone is immediately up and about, dropping dishes into the sink and threading arms through thick winter jackets. I claim my remaining slice of toast, grip it between my teeth, deposit my own plate with the others and climb into my jacket. Mum is doing the same, only she's looking at me and smiling. She doesn't speak but her eyes are pleased. I think she's glad we came. And I suppose I am too. Out here in the country, amongst these crusaders, my thoughts of Sam are fading from black to a slightly more bearable hue.

Outside the air is wet and wintry. The chill presses up against my cheeks like two cold hands. I breathe in deeply and feel a stab at the back of my throat. Exhaling creates a pale white mist and I watch as it disperses like magic into the icy atmosphere. Ahead of us the pale heavy sun is just clambering its way over the horizon. But its journey is slow and cautious. As it climbs higher the sky changes and brightens and sends the night-time shadows on their way. There's no more time for sleeping – the new day has arrived. It's still shiver-cold, but the light is warming and opening the world up for everyone to see.

All around me there are hills rolling with green grass and trees and shrubs with branches like bristles. Everywhere is wide open space. I breathe deeply once more. There's a faint smell of damp earth in the air. As the sun burns its shape onto my retinas my head feels as open as the great sky before me. The thoughts feel free. There's nothing crowding us in – not a single sight or sound. Everywhere is peaceful and still. And yet it all seems so alive. I can't translate it into words but today I feel a part of my surroundings, almost like I belong here amongst nature. Today I have purpose and the feeling is strangely uplifting.

'I can't see it, Frank,' Flora tut-tuts impatiently.

'It should be here any minute.'

'Wait a moment, I think I hear something…'

'That could be—'

'Would you shush!'

Frank does as he's told. But everything is silent, except for the sound of a slack-eyed Drew, sleepily massaging his morning stubble.

Scrape. Scrape.

Not even the birds are chirping.

Now there's a new, far-off sound. Rumble. Vroom.

'I think they're coming!'

And if it's a van pulling a horse trailer that Great Aunt Flora is after, then she's right. The towing vehicle carefully negotiates the potholes in the driveway and finally comes to a standstill only metres from where we're lingering expectantly. A bulky man wearing a cap and a thick padded jacket huffs his way out of the driver's seat and lumbers round to where we're all standing and waiting like this is a bus stop.

'Mornin'!'

'I almost thought you weren't coming, Tony,' Flora replies in a tone that's as frosty as the outside air.

'Yeah, well I had some trouble loading these geezers up,' Tony replies, jabbing a thick thumb at the trailer. 'A mind of their own, they have…'

Flora turns her cheek, evidently deciding to simply ignore the tardy man. 'Come along, everyone.' She claps her hands authoritatively. 'We've got two beautiful moos to welcome to Pips & Stones.' This is all the encouragement the New Faces, Mum and Frank need and everyone suddenly hops to the business of getting the horse trailer open. I remain where I am, munching on my now-cold slice of toast and fried tomato. Tony swaggers over to where I'm standing, eager to avoid any further involvement with the cows.

'So are you one of 'em foreigners who works for free?' he asks in his broad London accent.

I look at the man, surprised by his sudden proximity. There are faded tattoos climbing out of the sleeves and V-neck of his jacket. 'Er no, Flora is my great-aunt.'

'Ha, I didn't figure you for a hobbit lover.' He laughs like he's very funny.

'A what?'

'A hobbit lover. You know, one of 'em flaky wu-wu New Age sorts that wears cheesecloth and chants so as to become one with the universe.' He gives me a quick demonstration, bringing his fingers together and humming. 'Ommmm.'

'No, I'm not,' I reply.

Tony grins at me. There's a small gold star embedded in one of his front teeth. 'But my mum is.' The star disappears suddenly.

'Oh right. Well, Hare Krishna,' he says and ambles back over to his van.

Frank and Drew already have the doors of the horse trailer open while K'ya and Wil have climbed inside the vehicle in an attempt to push the animals out from the front. If the grunts and quiet curses are anything to go by, the cows aren't budging. Mum and Shawn Redd decide to find some treats to tempt the cows out while Flora positions herself at the rear of the cows, gently patting their bottoms.

'Come along you two, come along,' she croons in a motherly tone.

This is quite a show they're all putting on, the thoughts note as I pop the last bite of toast into my mouth and snuggle my hands deep inside my warm pockets. This could be entertaining.

'Liberty?' That's my great-aunt's voice.

'Uh-hmmm?' But I don't move; I don't want to encourage anybody here today.

'Could you give me a hand, dear girl?'

What, and rub a cow's backside? But I can't very well refuse so I slowly mooch my way over to the trailer with my hands still shoved in my pockets. Tony's grinning gold star is not lost on me.

'You stand on one side of this cow's rump,' Flora directs me, 'and I'll stand on the other side. K'ya and Wil at the front, push when I tell you. Now Libby, what you want to do is tug the beast along. Do you think you can do that?' I nod miserably. 'Right everyone, one, two, go!' We all do as we're told and for a few moments nothing of much consequence happens. The cow is certainly the stronger contestant. And then everything happens really quickly. Instead of reversing, the cow lifts its long paintbrush tail, which is only inches from my face, and lets rip with an almighty *shhhppppplll* sound. The stink quickly follows the sound – a hot sickly manure sort of smell. For a moment I simply stand there, shell-shocked and confused. I think the disgusting cow just farted in my face. And then Flora's head slowly emerges from the other side of the cow. She doesn't say anything; she doesn't have to. There's a bright green stripe running down the left side of her face.

I think they've all returned to the house. I can hear a substantial amount of banging and clanging coming from the kitchen: lunch is on the go, more than likely. But I don't bother leaving the sanctity of my brown batik giraffe bed. What's the point? I doubt anybody will be able to look at me without laughing out loud. Putting a hand over your mouth does nothing to muffle the laughter, the thoughts say. It's been hours since the flung dung incident, but I doubt anything will have changed. Of course Flora wasn't bothered in the slightest. She thought it was funny. But then she is married to Frank. I wonder if all farm folk are this batty? Too much fresh air, I suspect. Still, I don't care what anyone says, I wasn't happy. Having a cow's backside explode in my face is not 'nothing to be upset about'!

Knock knock.

Ah, finally Mum is coming to say sorry for her behaviour. She couldn't speak for at least five minutes afterwards.

Knock knock.

Still, I don't know why she's knocking on her own bedroom door.

'Just leave me alone!'

'It's Shawn. Do you think I could come in?'

Shawn Redd? Come in – what for? Does that mean she wants to talk to me? Why? We've barely exchanged two words. We've certainly never had a conversation. The girl makes me nervous. She stares.

'I, uh...I'm sleeping,' I reply, perhaps a little too forcibly for someone who's supposedly asleep. The door opens and Shawn Redd walks right in. I'm lying on my back with both feet propped up against the wall and a flower stick in each hand. 'Er...hello.' I quickly sit upright.

Shawn Redd looks up at me in the brown batik giraffe bed and rests her hands on her slender hips. 'What's that you're holding?' she asks.

I glance from my hands to her face. She's quite tall so I don't have to peer down too far to find her gaze. 'Uh, flower sticks.' But I don't offer an explanation. And Shawn Redd doesn't ask. But she does stare at them for a short while.

'So, are you feeling better?'

'I'm feeling cleaner,' I mumble. A bath in the bright bottle bathroom saw to that.

'Funny things happen to people all the time,' she says. 'You shouldn't take it too seriously. In the grand scheme of things, it really doesn't matter.'

I look down at Shawn Redd with her steep cheekbones, proud nose and thick ebony hair tied back in a stylish low ponytail and wonder if she had ever found herself on the receiving end of a cow's backside. I somehow doubt it. But she remains where she is, looking at me like she's considering me thoughtfully. I still don't say anything.

'You know, some people might consider what happened to you a sign of good luck.'

'I believe that's only if a bird does its business on you,' I glower haughtily from my giraffe-styled platform.

'Cow...bird...nature is nature.' Shawn Redd shrugs dismissively. 'Mind if I come up there and take a look at your flower sticks?'

That would make us feel very weird indeed, the thoughts grimace. But I give an outward shrug instead and Shawn Redd climbs her way to my level. I shift to the left to give her room and she claims it without hesitation or any degree of awkwardness.

'Where's the third stick?' she asks, pointing her dark eyeballs at the flower sticks still clutched in my fingers. I wordlessly hand her the third tasselled stick and she begins twirling it like a baton in her fingers. 'I haven't set eyes on flower sticks for ages.' She's smiling at me. 'I had a friend who was pretty good with these things.'

Yeah, me too. But I don't reply out loud and simply sit there feeling uncomfortable.

'And what's that over there?'

I follow her gaze. She's looking at the Victorian stereograph resting on top of my pillow.

'It's a three-dimensional Victorian stereograph.'

'Is that right. You've got some interesting things, Liberty Belle.'

'Libby,' I murmur. This is my sacred space and she's trespassing.

'Pardon?'

'It's Libby,' I repeat louder.

'And you can call me Shawn…it's just Shawn.' She's smiling softly.

As far as I can recall I don't think I've ever called her *anything*. It's the thoughts that keep calling her Shawn Redd.

'You've been through a tough time, Libby.' But she doesn't add anything further and leaves her words dangling unexplained in the air. Does she expect a reply?

'So my mum's been blabbing,' I finally sniff. *Again*. I'm annoyed. She had no right.

'Your mum hasn't mentioned a word, please believe me. I can see it – the sadness has taken the shape of your face.' Her gaze is gentle and without pity. There's a kindness about her eyes – a look that tells me it's OK to feel the way I do, that she understands.

I drop my chin to my chest and hide my sad face in the shadows. 'My best friend died,' I suddenly reveal without consciously setting out to do so. I expect to regret my words immediately but it feels strangely good to drop the act. Still, I hardly know Shawn Redd – or Shawn – although in some strange, inexplicable way it feels like I might have known her for ever, from another lifetime perhaps.

'The emptiness death leaves in its wake can be devastating,' she says quietly.

'I just miss him so much,' I nod and mumble, feeling the force of the emotion tumbling from me. For once I don't try to batten it down or keep it locked up tight inside me. There is something quietly reassuring and familiar about Shawn. This has nothing to do with the way she looks – I'm almost sure I'd remember her face, but there's something about the energy and light surrounding her that warms and holds me close. Maybe we're old souls, old friends from some other time.

She remains quietly thoughtful for a moment before continuing. 'It's a Native American belief that we are never left to suffer a tragedy alone. We believe that there is a divine strengthening influence – often something from nature – to remind us that the Creator is watching over us when we need it most.'

Her words are as sweet and smooth as hot cocoa, but I no longer understand.

'It might be a bird – a special messenger to let you know that you are cared for,' she explains. 'It may be a simple rainbow. It may be a burst of sunshine on a dark, cold day. Even a breeze reminds us that we're not alone.'

'I don't believe in God anymore,' I blurt out, even though Shawn said Creator, and not God. Does this mean different things to different people? Perhaps it doesn't really matter. For a while Shawn doesn't speak. Her eyes meet mine respectfully and gleam with warmth. Her gaze says as much as her lips. Today is about a heartfelt exchange of thoughts between friends.

'A great chief wrote that there is no death, only a change of worlds. Do you think it's possible that your friend is watching over you from another place?'

I dedicate some thought to this idea. Is it possible that Sam is still with me, and looking down on me – watching everything I do? I'd like that to be possible. Yes, the thought warms me considerably. Well, except the thought of him watching everything I do. *Everything?* Some things are private. But then Sam would know that; he'd respect my space. So all in all, the notion does make me feel better.

I smile at her for the first time. 'Thanks Shawn Re— uh, Shawn.'

The older girl doesn't acknowledge the thanks. Showing kindness is what people do for each other. 'Come on, we're going to debate what to name the cows. You don't want to miss it.' She smiles in a way that says, *trust me*! And in a strange, inexplicable way, I sort of already do.

We find everyone gathered outside the newly built cowshed lurking at the edge of a small field beyond the goats. They're considering something in loud, forceful tones and warming their gloved hands on the heat of their discussion.

'Each person is only allowed to nominate one name per cow,' Frank explains patiently for what I'm guessing is not the first time.

'Oh, hello Libby.' Flora greets me with her mind elsewhere. But she doesn't laugh at me and neither does anyone else. They're all thankfully too preoccupied, it seems, to laugh about the flung-dung incident any longer. Mum smiles and takes my mitten in hers. But she doesn't speak; I don't think Flora would appreciate the distraction.

'So do the cows have to have matching names?' Wil asks with a seriousness that belies the silliness of this conversation.

'Oh yes, very much so,' Flora clarifies. 'And I'd like them both to be named either after herbs or trees.'

'Does it have to be herbs or trees?' Drew wonders with a very solemn expression. I figure that he's taking this all very seriously until he catches my eye and gives me a small furtive wink and a grin that nobody else notices. He's enjoying this; he knows just how to get Flora and Frank going.

'Yes, how about capital cities instead – you know, like Tarawa and Dili?' Frank proposes bravely (or rather stupidly, according to the thoughts). He then surveys the group, wondering if everyone is duly impressed by his detailed geographical knowledge.

'Oh Frank!' Flora shakes her head in irritation. 'Trees or herbs, I won't be swayed.' Perhaps the cows are essentially Flora's and the goats belong to Frank. That might explain his beard. 'Right, we'll begin with you, Iris, and move clockwise. What do you say?'

'Rosemary and Coriander,' Mum replies with confidence. Flora tilts her head from left to right – the suggestion isn't half bad. Now she's looking pointedly at Drew.

'Uh, I like the name Herb,' he says determinedly. But he doesn't look at Flora; he knows he's being reckless. Still, he'll push the boundaries for Frank because sticking together is what guys do.

'Herb is a boy's name.' Flora dismisses his suggestion without pointing to the fact that Herb is not actually the name of a herb. 'Wil?'

'Willow and Ash.'

'I like Violet and Betony,' suggests Shawn.

'Mint and Mugwort,' K'ya grins.

Frank is tight-lipped. 'Pass,' he replies sulkily.

'Libby?' Flora's ignoring her husband and staring at me.

'Uh, pass too.' But I'm thinking Mad Cow and Butthead.

'Well, thank you for those suggestions, one and all,' Flora begins thoughtfully, 'but what about Parsley and Patchouli.' But this doesn't sound like a question or another suggestion at all.

'Like we'll even be able to tell the cows apart,' Frank murmurs sullenly.

'I certainly will. It's obvious which is which,' says Flora.

'It's not obvious to me,' Frank retorts.

Suddenly everyone begins talking at once, layering one sentence over the next until the air is a cacophony of loudly voiced opinions. I glance over at Shawn who catches my eye, smiles and winks. She was right – I'm glad I didn't miss this. I may have been the victim of bovine bum, but at least I'm not arguing over what to call a pair of daft cows. Like animals really care what they're called anyway.

The air outside is as dark and empty as a black hole even though it's only gone four-thirty in the afternoon. With the animals locked up safe and snug and the plants sheltered from the winter frost by the protective plastic sheeting of the polytunnel, the human beings at Pips & Stones are finally all huddled inside the straw house. And this is where we'll stay for the rest of the evening, if we have any sense. The wood burner in the corner of the living room is glowing gold and hot and there's the smell of sizzling onions lingering in the air. Flora is preparing stew for our supper; Frank is her downtrodden but resolute helper.

'I still think Parsley is a silly name for a cow,' he says, standing his ground with his jaw tipped in defiance.

'And you call Tarawa and Dili memorable?'

I'm sitting and watching the verbal volleys like this is Wimbledon for words. This is exactly what happens when you don't have a television set, the thoughts observe. They are profound sometimes.

'Look what I've discovered!' That's Wil, and she's

carrying a square, brown cardboard box and clucking with delight.

Nobody seems to recognise the box so she places it on the floor and rummages inside for its contents. She extracts a string of pinecones bound to a long silver thread like a magician pulling a rabbit from a hat. Ta da.

'Cool, dude – last year's Christmas decorations!' Drew cheers.

Suddenly everyone is interested and scurrying for the box. Everyone except for me, that is. I'm still boycotting Christmas.

'Oh look, the baubles I made from recycled light bulbs!' K'ya is holding up a selection of brightly coloured glass ornaments for all to see.

'And the paper chains we slaved over,' adds Shawn with a smile, draping a series of interlinked colourful paper hoops around her neck like a scarf.

'Ah, the cottonwool snowballs,' sighs Wil nostalgically, gently dropping a handful over my head so that I'm caught in a very brief snowstorm. 'You look wonderfully Christmassy already, Libby!' she says, smiling brightly at me. 'Come on everyone, let's decorate the tree.'

I still haven't moved. I'm obviously the only one who's taken note of the fact that we have no Christmas tree. But before I can bah-humbug point to this little fact, everyone is suddenly gathered around the tree growing in the middle of the straw house. Silly me, I should have known. I also wasn't expecting this spiritual lot to be interested in the distinctly Christian event known as Christmas.

Flora quickly takes up directing traffic from the pot of stew on the stove. 'Shawn, don't forget last year's foil flowers. And Libby, be a dear and fetch the shoebox of ribbons from the cupboard near the bathroom. You can wrap the ribbons around the trunk of the tree – tie them with bows. It'll look smashing.'

My great-aunt seems intent on getting me involved in all her little projects. The last one blew up in my face. Literally. And yet I still don't have the courage to refuse her, even if I have silently boycotted the festive season. There are only three days left until Christmas Day; I thought I'd gotten away with it. I really believed that I had managed to avoid the stupid event. But I fetch the ribbons anyway because it's the least complicated of all the options available to me.

For a while there are too many people gathered around the tree for me to make my mark with the fabric trimmings. Of course I don't mind. I view decorating this tree exactly as I do feeding those pot-bellied goats a pitchfork full of hay: it's simply something that is expected of me. When you're a teenager this list can seem endless. But I'm in no hurry. Only when the string of pinecones has been strung, and the recycled painted light bulbs hung, do I finally amble over to the garnished foliage with my box of ribbons. Everybody else has moved on from decorating the tree to preparing the table for our stew dinner. So I sit down quietly on the floor at the base of the tree and begin sifting through the ribbons. First I sort them into colours; my plan is to have them evenly spaced. And then I begin wrapping the ribbons around the trunk of the tree, joining each one end to end, with a bow, as per my great-aunt's supportive but firm suggestion.

'It looks lovely.'

I don't have to turn around to recognise Shawn's voice. 'Thanks,' I reply, still facing forwards.

There's a shuffling beside me, I think she's sitting down too. I swivel my eyeballs far left and spy her fiddling with the ribbons I have set out in sequence. She hands me the next one in line. 'Bet you've never decorated a tree quite like this one, huh?' She laughs gently.

'No, not quite.' I accept the proffered ribbon without enthusiasm.

'Something tells me you're not Christmas-mad.'

No, just a general sort of mad, the thoughts offer as an

alternative. 'I think it's a hypocritical holiday.' I shrug, like *who cares.* And how come Shawn seems to be able to read the thoughts?

'I do see your point,' she nods. 'But if it encourages people to show a little more goodwill towards one another, even if just for a short while, then perhaps Christmas is not all bad.'

'I guess.' Repeat shrug. I can't imagine Native Americans decorating their tepees with tinsel, somehow. Come to think of it, I doubt they actually live in tepees anymore. But I can't imagine them decorating their houses either.

'So what *do* you believe in, Libby?' She knows I don't believe in God or Christmas. Perhaps, like me, she's wondering what's left for me in this world.

'I believe in the Peace Project.' My voice does not falter.

'Oh right?' She sounds interested. 'So tell me about it.'

And I do. I explain that the Peace Project is an international peace movement intended to spread the message of peace, love and acceptance around the world. I tell her that there is a group of Peace Project volunteers stationed in every single country around the world (of which there are 193, I add authoritatively), and on New Year's Day a prayer for peace will cover the entire planet. I tell her that the entire event has been carefully calculated and orchestrated so that by the end of the first day of the New Year the entire planet will be blessed by a prayer for peace. It will filter through every country, infusing the air and hearts and minds of its people with thoughts of harmony and love. I know this last part almost by heart.

Shawn is silent and still, but I barely even notice. I'm wading through my memories of Sam. He was so passionate about the Peace Project, like it was everything we needed to save the world. I stare down at the silky ribbons in my hands and wonder if his faith and willpower alone could have brought an end to war. Sam could have changed the world. He would have, too. I'm not the only one who lost something on the day he died.

'That's a very good thing to believe in,' is all Shawn finally says. If she's noticed the teardrops spreading like oily stains across the threads of ribbons now wound tightly around my fingers she doesn't show it. If she recognises that the Peace Project is only something to believe in for now – that from the second of January I will have nothing else to occupy my heart and mind – then she doesn't let on either. For now she keeps quiet, as if this organised universal prayer for peace is enough to sustain me spiritually, like it's big and bright enough to fill the empty space left in my life by the departure of God and the birth of His only son, and the death of my best friend. For now we're both pretending that the first day of the New Year is an all-you-can-eat buffet for the soul.

If anyone else notices our sombre mood-change they don't let on. Flora is still stirring her stew and scolding Frank for misplacing last year's Christmas wreath made out of the holly she'd carefully collected, all on her own, out in the cold, drizzle-drenched countryside. Frank is searching for the necessary spices to make mulled wine and quite obviously trying to pretend that Flora is still outside, in the cold, searching for her holly. Mum, Wil and K'ya are stringing popcorn and discussing the origins of various Christmas carols. The only one who doesn't appear to be consumed by this concentrated explosion of festive spirit is Drew, whose ear has been replaced by a small black portable radio. His socked feet, which were tapping the floor, are suddenly motionless – toes pointing north.

'Hey, dudes!' We're all suddenly silent. Drew is pitched forward, pressing the radio to the side of his face and staring at the air in front of his eyes. 'Listen up! They predict snow for tonight.'

In an instant everyone is babbling excitedly. Everyone except for Flora, that is. She's standing with her arms crossed, the hand gripping the stew spoon drip-dripping onto the wooden kitchen floor.

'Pah! They say that every year,' she says, loud enough to make herself heard.

Drew is still listening intently to the radio. 'No really, Flora,' he replies earnestly, 'there's talk about a moving band of pressure bringing wind and snow from Russia or something.' He pauses for a moment. 'Yup, they can almost guarantee snow tonight!' He looks jubilant, like it's something he's been saying all along.

'That means we wake up to a winter wonderland wrapped up in white.' K'ya grins happily.

Wil is quickly infected by her mood. 'How about we plan a walk straight after breakfast tomorrow morning?' Now everyone is grinning.

'Brill!'

'We could head through the forest up to the river.'

'We'll wrap up really warm.'

'It'll be beautiful!'

Flora still appears doubtful but for once doesn't say anything. Everyone else looks really pleased so it must be decided. I haven't cast my vote but the thoughts and I are looking forward to this walk for one reason and one reason only: it means we can escape stupid Christmas and all these irritating decorations.

I've been sitting, curled up, watching the world outside turn from black to white. I was the first person awake this morning – probably a one-time-only record since my arrival at Pips & Stones. I opened my eyes and listened quietly for a counted minute just to be sure that nobody else had beaten me to it, and only then did I slip from my warm nest beside Mum, whose breathing was still deep and heavy with sleep. I walked soundlessly on imaginary high heels through to the lounge and set myself down with a blanket in front of one of the straw house windows. I don't know why, but I wanted to be the first to watch the whiteness seep through the darkness like a developing film negative. At first everything was blind black. And then a dim light just beyond the horizon clicked on. It grew gradually brighter until finally the whiteness emerged through the shadows like a dazzling debutante at dawn.

But I haven't moved. I'm still sitting in front of the window, cloaked in the same blanket, staring out at a bleached world with soft organic contours. The view is breathtaking. The countryside has been reduced to its most basic forms, without colour or distracting decoration, to be appreciated for its shape and simplicity. But the peace and quiet will end soon; I can hear the house stirring.

'There you are, darling.' That's Mum and she kisses me good morning. I notice that she's already dressed. The only thing missing from her outfit is her shoes which are, more specifically, slightly muddy boots currently dangling from her fingers. I'm about to tell her about the darkness turning to white when a dozen feet suddenly stomp their way from the bedroom end of the straw house into the living room, where I'm still curled up in the comfort of my blanket.

'Liberty, you're not even dressed yet!' Flora is staring down at me with her hands pinching her hips. 'Come on girl, we're about ready to leave for our walk.'

Nobody else bothers me; they're all too busy searching for things I suspect might be hats, gloves and scarves. 'I thought we were having breakfast first?' My hungry belly thought so too.

Flora punches the air enthusiastically and begins talking and walking in the direction of the kitchen. 'Ah, plan change! I thought we might have breakfast along the way. I've already made us a batch of vegetarian-sausage sandwiches and egg and spinach frittatas.'

'We're going to eat them cold?' Drew looks perturbed and delivers a grimace in my general direction. We are partners in the pursuit of a hot breakfast.

Flora doesn't dignify this with a response and busies herself packing a couple of backpacks with the wrapped food and flasks of what could be tea or coffee.

'Are you going out dressed like that?' This time it's Frank who is leaning over me with his knuckles pressed against his thin waist.

'No.' I sigh and exhale through O lips. But I don't ditch the warm blanket; I pull it tighter around me and make a trail down the corridor towards the bedroom I share with Mum.

It only takes me a few moments to throw some layers on – I don't care what I look like, I just want to be warm. And after a short trip to the bathroom I'm back in the living room with breath that smells of peppermint. 'I'm ready,' I announce to those who may have missed the appearance of my fully clothed self.

'What shoes are you wearing?' Flora asks.

The thoughts wonder if this is a trick question. What does the great-aunt think the dung-stained trainers attached to the laces hooked through my fingers are for?

I hoist the shoes slightly higher in the air to make it clearer.

'You can't wear those things.'

'Why not?' I know they're disgusting but if her farm animals didn't go so much—

'They're not waterproof, that's why. Those things won't last a mile in the snow.' I really wish she'd stop calling my shoes *those things*. I stare at her vacantly. 'Here…' Flora turns and disappears for a moment. 'You can wear these boots – they're my spare pair.' She's proffering a couple of old brown leather boots. I can't take my eyes off them. Years of wear have moulded the discoloured leather into the precise shape – bunions, lumps and all – of Flora's old knotted feet. I feel green.

'I don't think so!' That was a talking thought broken free.

'Why ever not?' My great aunt looks offended. I'm trying to ignore K'ya who is standing behind Flora and smiling at me compassionately (but looks very close to exploding with laughter).

'They're uh, too big.' Flora is, after all, taller than me.

'Nonsense,' she caws, 'I've got surprisingly small feet. What size are you?'

I remain quiet. I know what size I am; I'm trying to figure out what size she's not. 'A…uh…size six?'

'Perfect! I'm a six-and-a-half, which means you'll have a little extra room for thick socks.'

The joy.

'I've got a spare pair of super-thick socks you could borrow – they'll keep you warm,' offers Frank.

That should conclude my misery. How about I use them to hang myself instead, the thoughts grimace. 'No thanks,' I mumble aloud and quickly shove my woollen beanie onto my head and pull it low so that my view is partially obscured. I need to pretend that this isn't happening to me, even if just for a brief moment. Mum lifts the hat slightly and hands me a pair of my own socks with a look that says 'sorry, darling, but it could be worse'. But I don't know what could be worse than being forced to wear your ancient great-aunt's sweat-stained knobbly boots.

'Are we all ready?' Flora is scrutinising everyone up and down while I breathe deep and sentence my feet to the boots. Theoretically my skin is touching the socks and not the actual boots, the thoughts repeat feverishly. But I can feel the indents of Flora's toes in the soles of the boots. Gnarly old great-aunt toes. Eeugh. Sometimes I really wish the thoughts would just shut it.

I'm the last one out of the front door. Everyone is

loitering in the drive while Drew consults a map dangling in the air.

'I know the route – there's no need for a map,' Flora barks authoritatively.

'That's just as well,' says Shawn, 'because he had the thing upside down.' She winks at me and grins broadly.

'Er, did not,' Drew grumbles but quickly folds the broad sheet of paper up again. Flora's all-business and quickly takes the lead while Frank does a little canter to catch her up. The rest of us fall in haphazardly behind the determined pair and for the first time begin to absorb the whitewashed world around us. The air feels arctic and pure as it hits my lungs like a jet stream. At first the sensation is almost painful, but soon the vigour of fresh air in my lungs is revitalising.

The day is still crisp and new and everywhere is soft and sublime. This is like a giant marshmallow world. Of course I've seen snow before, quite a few times, but I've never been out in the countryside surrounded by snow. I really only know two places – Manchester and Brighton – neither of which are particularly countrified. I'm more used to an artificial environment of bricks and concrete – man-made stuff. There's always been the ocean, but that's completely different. I haven't done much more than sit at her edges. But the countryside is a three-dimensional world I can disappear into and explore.

Pips & Stones has already disappeared behind the winter bristles of a line of tall trees. Up ahead is a hill with a path running alongside a hedge of stout shrubs. I only know there's a path because animals – I'm guessing sheep or cows – have already walked a trail in the snow. Things will probably be different once we reach the top of the hill but for now, no matter where I look, I'm surrounded by a world that's all natural. For now there's not a single building, road, fence, bus or car, neon sign, telephone pole, street light or stained pavement in sight. Everything is wide open and untouched. There are no crowds or noise. There's simply space and peaceful silence. Of course I have Mum and the others just a few steps away, but for the time being they're also quiet and searching this world where nothing is filled in or painted over or bricked up. Nothing matches, is perfectly spaced or measures a perfect angle. In this world nothing is controlled or directed. Nothing happens quickly; life just ambles along at its own curvy, quirky pace. And for the first time I feel a connection to the planet beneath my feet encased in Flora's knobbly boots.

The higher up the hill we climb the bigger the

trees – once unnoticeable – appear to grow. It's only when we're close to the summit that I realise we're at the edge of a woodland made dense by trees standing fast and firm in soil turned black by the wet decaying leaves left over from autumn. Mum stops walking and locks her hands behind her head. Her breathing is deep and drawn out.

'I'm not as young as I once was,' she smiles at me. 'Or as fit!' Her face is a whiter shade of pale with crimson patches for cheeks. Drew and the girls reply with compassionate grins also battling for breath. Flora and Frank, on the other hand, remain sturdy and silent.

'Young folk.' Flora tut-tuts and rolls her sinewy shoulders like she's an athlete. Frank doesn't look quite as cool but he seems determined to live the lie. Flora would get too much mileage out of a show of weakness.

The heavens above have, up until now, remained a milky churning mass we've largely been ignoring. We don't seem to notice the shifting clouds until a sudden burst of brilliant blue sky catches us all completely unawares. The bright light dilutes the shadows and, almost instantly, melts the greyness, leaving our small group basking in a glorious glow that transforms the snowy whiteness into a bank of glittering crystals. Looking from the sky to the captivated faces of the people around me, I realise that this walk is no longer simply a country ramble. My new friends and family suddenly seem uplifted and optimistic, like everything is beautiful and anything is possible. They look like they're having a spiritual experience.

'Tell me there's not a God.' Wil breathes in deeply and lifts her face to the corner of heaven poking through the clouds. I glance quickly at Shawn and then back at Wil, suddenly suspicious and then no longer sure. Has Shawn been sharing my secrets? But Wil said the words so softly I don't think she meant them for anyone but herself.

Flora and Frank have already moved on and we all do the same. We enter the forest and the light follows us, seeping through the naked winter trees. Soft sunlight envelops the jagged branches, still crusty with snow that has fallen at an angle, painting single white stripes across dark wet bark. A few of the boughs still carry nests long since abandoned by warm-blooded birds flown south for the winter. There's a wide space weaving its way through the trees and Flora seems to be following it. This time there are no animal tracks to highlight the path. Not that she needs their help, I'm sure.

As the sun grows stronger the finer deposits of snow

are the first to melt, creating dripping branches that hang like chandeliers. I reach out a hand, snatch a drop and lift it to my lips. It's water, that's all. It just looked so magical.

We cross a small wooden swing-bridge that's suspended less than a metre or so above soft ground that looks thick and boggy. Once past the marshy clearing the assembly of trees soon continues. Flora and Frank have come to a standstill up ahead. It takes us a few moments to catch them up and when we do I notice that they're standing beside a slatted wooden bench with curved metal legs. There's a plaque attached to the backrest. I move closer to read its inscription.

In memory of Simon,
Always our inspiration.
J.G. & D.G. x

I read it once more. There's something very special about dedicating something to someone you love, especially if all you have left of them are memories. It's almost like, thanks to this bench, a small part of this Simon continues to exist in our world. But the sentiment seems to have been lost on Drew, who has begun grumbling about breakfast – or lack thereof. So

I put the thoughts of dedications away for later. But I'm suddenly feeling optimistic. If anybody deserves a dedication it's definitely my best friend Sam. I might just do it for the both of us.

'We're almost at the river,' Flora says, speaking directly to Drew. 'Do you think you can wait?'

Drew places an open palm on his flat belly and considers the question for a moment. He nods. And so off we all trudge once more, heading for what I'm guessing is the river.

I hear it before I see it. The sound sneaks into the ether – a soft gurgling sort of noise that slowly becomes a louder sloshing echo that reminds me of how much I need the toilet (even if I hadn't consciously realised it). Unfortunately I don't spy a convenient sanitised portaloo anywhere nearby.

'What do you do if you need to go to the toilet?' I whisper to Mum.

'A number one or two?' she whispers her reply.

'Oh yuk, Mum. I just need to wee.' This break in the country is beginning to take on a theme.

'I guess you just find a tree. Let me ask Flora.'

'Oh-please-no!' (*Like I want the entire world to find out.*) 'Just forget it.'

'There's a lake up ahead,' Frank suddenly speaks for

the first time. 'It's a scenic spot to pause for breakfast.' He smiles kindly at Drew, his one and only buddy in all things non-female.

And Frank's right, it is scenic, except the lake is really more of a large pond. Smooth round stones cling to its edges and descend into the dark still water, which can't be very deep, not if the log sticking out of the centre of the pond – or lake – is any sort of yardstick. I take this opportunity to quickly disappear behind a mound obscured by shrubbery. And when I return a short while later everyone is milling around the water's edge drinking steamy tea from beakers and munching on wrapped herb sausage sandwiches. Drew is the first to finish and quickly finds a small flat pebble, which he then expertly skims across the water's opaque surface. The stone bounces three times before sinking. He's started something. Soon everyone is having a go – even Mum. But I don't have the urge. I find myself a sandwich and a beaker and watch from the sidelines, smiling at my mum's dismal attempts. I never realised it before, but the part of her brain in charge of physical co-ordination quite obviously has an *Out of Order* sign hanging from it.

'I'm guessing she hasn't won any pebble-skimming championships lately.'

I turn to the voice, even though I recognise it as belonging to Shawn. She's standing beside me, staring out across the water and also smiling at Mum's hopeless efforts. I laugh but don't say anything. Flora finishes her sandwich, de-crumbs her hands on her jeans and joins the skimmers at the water's edge. She unsurprisingly takes a very competitive approach to the business of pebble skimming, and as a result of her exuberant efforts, Drew almost lands headfirst into the cold murky water.

'She's not a bad sort,' Shawn speaks again. 'Flora, I mean. She can be a bit bossy, but she has a very good heart.'

'I know.' I nod and shove my now sandwich-free hand inside a warm pocket.

'How about you and I collect some holly – there's loads of it about. We could surprise Flora with another Christmas wreath for the front door. I know Frank would be grateful to hear the last of the missing wreath of Christmas past. Ha ha.'

I'm not laughing though. 'Shawn, can I ask you something?'

'Sure.'

'If we don't go to church and Flora and Mum always bang on about being spiritual rather than religious and

K'ya reads the Koran' – I saw it sticking out of her bag – 'then how come we're all celebrating Christmas?'

'You mean why are we decorating the tree?'

I shrug and nod at the same time.

'Actually, I think Drew is Christian,' Shawn considers thoughtfully, 'not that he says much on the subject. Faith can be a very personal thing. But in answer to your question, we decorate the tree to be festive, I suppose. And perhaps, in our own special way, we're also acknowledging Christianity, the main religion of Great Britain. This country is, after all, our home for the moment. And isn't love and acceptance and kinship what being religious is really all about?'

But I won't be sidetracked. 'So do you believe in God?'

Shawn pauses and breathes deeply. 'Religion is quite often simply an accident of birth, if you think about it. For example, if you're born into an Islamic family, you'll probably be raised to believe in Allah. Have you ever wondered, if you were born in a different country, what your religion might have been?'

Theoretically, since I've given up on God, I don't belong to any religion so there's no sense in wondering – it doesn't really matter where I might have been born. But I don't want to disappoint Shawn so I make an attempt to think about it quietly for a moment anyway. And still not very much makes sense. 'Uh, I guess. But what do *you* believe in?' Today I am persistent, I need answers.

'Well, I believe there is a Spirit – a loving energy that moves through all things, including you and me. If I sit quietly and watch the natural world around me – that is the trees, the birds in the trees, the clouds in the sky…I believe it's possible to see and feel the Spirit at work in all of these things. It brings me a sense of fulfilment and peace. I suppose this is my experience of God. When you remove obstacles and listen quietly in a world without man-made intrusion, it's easier to experience God's presence. And perhaps even your own presence too. This Spirit – or God – is not contained in a building you visit or a book you must read. It is not separate from you or me. All the goodness that exists inside us – that is God. Because you are part of God. This is your spirituality.'

But Shawn's not quite done explaining. 'Religion, on the other hand,' she continues thoughtfully, 'has almost become a badge of identity we wear. But we're really not as different as we might think. The different religions actually have a lot in common. To begin with, most agree that a Spirit, by whatever name – God, Allah,

Buddha, it doesn't matter – exists. And most will tell you that love is the ultimate goal of their faith. Basically the essence of any religion is a good heart. Or it's supposed to be, anyway. So perhaps we should simply think of the various religions as different paths leading to the same goal. Love and compassion really are the universal religion. And religion is just an extension of our spirituality.'

I listen to what Shawn has to tell me and look around at the peaceful beauty of the surrounding nature. I know I said I've given up on God but today I feel a stirring inside me. I do feel a part of something great and quite magnificent. But it's still not enough.

'Libby?'

My eyes are burning.

'Are you thinking about your friend, Sam?'

I dip my head. The thoughts are always thinking about Sam.

'Nobody can say for sure why Sam died and you didn't, Libby. But nobody is being punished. Some people believe that the human soul lives on forever, but we all know that the human body does not. We are designed with physical limitations. And while the world jostles and churns around us sometimes we don't survive the commotion. That's part of nature too.

Perhaps it really is that simple.'

I'm looking down, staring right past Flora's knobbly old boots. I have a lot to think about. I haven't forgotten my conversation with Mum outside the church on the cliff, after Sam's funeral. I said that religion had made the world crazy. I said that everybody believed that their religion was the right one and hated those who believed otherwise. Mum felt that maybe this had everything to do with our being human and very little to do with God. When I'm done thinking about this I lift my head and smile appreciatively at Shawn through eyeballs half-filled with water.

'So I guess dying makes us human and not God, huh?' I finally reply.

'I want to go home.' I keep my voice so low it barely strums my vocal chords. My words are nothing more than warm air in Mum's ear.

'What do you mean?' Her voice is no louder than mine.

'I want to return to Brighton.' I don't know why we're whispering; we're the only ones in the bedroom, wrapped up warm and cosy and protected by the brown batik giraffes lying sentry.

'I thought you were enjoying Pips & Stones. You seemed to be settling in.'

'It's OK.' I shrug. I suppose I do look forward to each day a little more, but I still feel guilty. The thoughts think it might be too soon. 'There's just something I have to do back in Brighton. And I have to get it done before New Year's Day.' I don't fill in the blanks with details, even though it's unlikely this speck of information will be enough to convince Mum. She remains quiet and thoughtful in the shadows before delivering her verdict.

'Flora is expecting us to stay for lunch. Tomorrow is Christmas Day, after all. How about we leave the morning after – on Boxing Day instead?'

I wait for the 'but': a demand from Mum for an explanation as to why I want to return home so suddenly. But she remains silent. She seems to trust me enough to forego an interrogation. Perhaps she knows that I wouldn't ask if it wasn't very important to me. Mum always did understand me better than anyone. This reminds me of just how much I love her. I wiggle closer, pressing my shape into hers.

'Thanks Mum,' I whisper. I then close my eyes and fall into a deep, dreamless sleep.

My body may still be at Pips & Stones but my heart and mind are already back in Brighton. I've got so much to ponder and plan that Christmas Day – the day I've been dreading for ages – passes me by in a rather insignificant but not entirely unpleasant blur. We all slept late this morning. My guess is we were all exhausted from yesterday's long walk through the countryside. But we finally stirred and straightened, one by one, and warmed ourselves with chocolate hot off the stove while Flora fussed over pots and pans sizzling with caramelised parsnips and baby onions, nut roast braised with cranberry chutney, roasted home-grown potatoes, wild mushroom crêpes and spiced winter pudding soaked in cinnamon cream. We then settled in around the worn table and ate and drank and seemed to enjoy each other's company as much as the delicious food.

As usual everyone had so much to say I really didn't have to make much effort. But I listened – or I tried to, anyway – when the thoughts weren't debating loudly in my head (New Year's Day is only a few days away, was their constant reminder). Now I'm sitting in a pool of yesterday's blanket with Christmas Day almost behind me and a plate of buttermilk biscuits resting in front of me. I'm nibbling and I'm thinking.

K'ya and Drew are the first to find me and my quiet spot. I quickly offer up the plate of biscuits, guiltily wiping the crumbs from my lips. I've eaten practically the entire lot.

'We've come to say goodnight.' The older girl shakes her head at the biscuits but smiles down at me. 'Your mum says you're leaving early tomorrow morning, so I suppose this is goodbye too.'

'Oh right,' I mumble through biscuit and make a move to untangle myself from the blanket. But K'ya is quicker and touches each one of my cheeks with her lips before I can break free. I do have one available arm though and I attempt to hug her with it. But the gesture seems stiff. I'm no good at goodbyes; I think I've just said the word too many times.

'Your mum says that we might see you again – same place, same time next year. That would be lovely.'

I give the blanket one last tug. It's no good; I think I'm sitting on the end bit. 'Yes, that would be brilliant,' I smile awkwardly.

Drew steps forward and gives my head a rub. 'It was great to meet you, Libbo.'

'Yes, we're definitely going to miss you, Libby.' That was Wil, who is suddenly standing beside Drew and K'ya and flanked by Shawn, who also seems to have made a sudden and unexpected appearance. I'm starting to feel uncomfortable, not least because I remain trapped by the wretched blanket with my head angled at groin height. Group goodbyes don't do me much good either.

'I'm, uh, definitely going to miss you guys too,' I mumble. And I really will.

Wil bends forward to hug me. 'Take care, sweetheart.'

'Yeah, you be good.'

'See you in one year.'

'Keep recycling!'

And then they're gone – everyone except for Shawn, that is. She's still standing there. 'This is for you,' she says and hands me a book bound in large pressed leaves.

'What's this for?' I open it, it's empty inside.

'It's just a place for you to write down your thoughts. I figured it might help you to make sense of them.'

I wonder how the thoughts will feel about being committed to paper; they usually like to roam free and unfettered. But I'm willing to try most things. 'Thanks very much,' I smile.

'I wrote my email address on the very last page,' she adds. 'I'd love to keep hearing more of your thoughts too.' Now she's smiling.

A year would be a very long time to wait to tell Shawn about what I have in mind and I'm suddenly grateful for her address. It's too early to share the thoughts with her just yet, but I think she'll be very pleased when I do tell her that I believe I've finally found a way to move forward with my life. Even better news yet is that I think I know how to do this with Sam's memory held close to my side.

twenty-two
the right thing to do

A bell chimes and Mum is the first to reach the door. That's probably because I haven't budged a millimetre. I'm still sitting cross-legged on the futon in Mum's little cottage on Brighton's coast. And I'm suddenly feeling very nervous. Perhaps this wasn't such a good idea after all.

'How are you, Gloria?' I hear Mum ask.

'I'm getting on with things day by day,' is the reply. I can't see Gloria but of course I recognise her voice. It hasn't been that long. 'How was your time with Flora and Frank?'

'It was what we needed, I think. They were very good to us and appeared sad to wave us goodbye. But it's good to be home again.' Now there's a short awkward silence. 'Uh, how about a cup of tea? Libby should be out in a moment.'

I take this as my cue and breathe deeply before carefully unfolding my legs. I can't hide away forever, especially since it was my idea to invite Gloria in the first place. I find her standing alone in the lounge, staring out of the window at the ocean with her eyes narrowed. I don't know that she'll ever forgive the diva.

'Hello Gloria.'

The small woman spins in fright, recognises my face and quickly swaps her fear for a subtle but sincere smile. 'Oh, Libby. Sorry love, you startled me. How are you?'

'Fine. How are you?'

She doesn't reply but simply shrugs and nods her head as if to say, 'It's going to take time.'

Just then Mum reappears with a tray of teacups. 'I found Lotus's secret stash of ginger biscuits,' she says, plugging the air with the sound of trivial chit-chat. 'They're good for dunking.' Next she mentions her obsession with dunking oatmeal rusks before reliving the wonderful views from Pips & Stones for us. I sit there listening to her natter, wondering if this means that we've progressed to the next stage of grief: where it's OK to acknowledge that life outside of our sorrow continues to exist. It might seem insignificant to outsiders, but being able to value the wonders of a good dunking biscuit is a positive sign of the healing process. I begin to feel a little more confident.

'Gloria,' I say, clearing my throat. And then I remember Mum's unwavering trust in me. 'And Mum,' I add, catching her gaze for a moment, 'I want to talk to you about something. You see, I've had an idea. It's about Sam.' I notice Gloria's eyelids flutter at the mention of his name, like somebody pinched her but she's refusing to howl. Perhaps she's not quite as far along the grieving process as I'd first thought. Still, it's too late to turn back now.

'The thing is…Sam's the best person I've ever known. He cared so much about people – and the world. He made it a better place. Given the chance, he really could have changed the world.' I sense that I'm rambling but I can't seem to rein my words in and force them to walk at a sedate, comprehensible pace. 'He cared about so many things…about the International Peace Project especially. He really put his heart and soul into it. So I thought…I figured…we could…we should dedicate our prayer for peace to Sam…you know…and send out our prayer on the wings of Sam's memory.'

I pause at this moment to assess the effect my words are having on my audience. Gloria looks slightly stunned, Mum looks pensive. I'm not sure if this is good or bad but I have a general rule that when in doubt, just keep on going. And besides, I would find it very difficult to turn away from this idea now. Immortalising Sam *is* my healing process.

'Of course I know that it's not just up to us…I realise

there are 192 other countries involved in the Project. But Sam knew practically every single Project organiser in just about every single country. OK...so he never *knew* them...but he spent endless hours on email...making contact with so many people. And so many people knew Sam. And they loved him just like we do. If anyone's a personification of peace, it's definitely Samir Pejic.'

Both women are still looking at me closely. Neither has spoken. They're simply staring. In my head I imagined them interrupting my presentation with shrieks of enthusiasm and eager ideas of their own to add to the pot. I expected whoops of excitement. But so far, nothing. My show has been rained on by disinterest. It's turned wet outside too. The black skies have finally opened; the window panes instantly blistering with swollen beads of water that slide slowly south.

'So, uh, what do you both think?' I finally ask. Mum is the first to respond.

'Well, I...' She glances from me to Gloria for confirmation. I can see that she thinks it's a good idea. And she's glowing, proud of the fact that I thought it up. But she appears nervous in front of Gloria. Mum is always careful around people's feelings; it's just how she is. And if I know her as well as I believe I do, then she's considering two particular things right now. The first is that it doesn't really matter what she thinks, my idea has to earn the approval of Gloria before anyone else. And secondly, she doesn't feel that it's right for her to wear her motherly pride on her face, not in front of her grieving friend anyway. So Mum empties her face and waits patiently for Gloria to respond.

I set out with brisk optimism, but now I'm starting to slump with worry. The rain is making splat sounds on the window pane. Thoughts of a Peace Project dedication to Sam's memory have been feeding my soul for days now. Of course I always knew that my idea would require Gloria's blessing but for some reason I simply assumed she would grant it. I never allowed myself to think thoughts to the contrary. After all, what would I do then? How would I get through days of sunrises and sunsets, with no Sam in between? Without a Plan B, a Peace Project dedication to Sam's memory has almost become my reason for being. But now here I sit, staring ahead into the heavy silence, waiting for an answer.

But then Gloria's face begins slowly to change. It starts to brighten and open up like a flower in springtime. There's even the suggestion of a smile pressing apostrophe shapes into the corners of her mouth. She looks me in the eye and eventually caves into a smile.

'Liberty Belle, I think that's a wonderful idea!' She finally seems excited, and now that she's grabbed a firm hold of the idea she's quickly filtering through the details. Her eyes dart left to right while she ties knots in her fingers and mentally prepares a To Do list. 'Of course there are all of our Peace Project friends to consider in this too. Every one of our own Project colleagues knew Sam; I've had messages from most of them already. But we have to get the support of every single country too. We've got to do this properly for it to count! And that's a whole lot of emails to send out. We haven't got much time either. But if we pull together we can make it work.' She pauses to breathe what might just be her first deep breath since Sam died.

'I'll help too,' Mum quickly joins in, looking equally energised. 'And I know that Lotus would love to play a part. Whatever needs doing, we'll be there!'

This means we have a dedicated team of four; there's no stopping us now. I feel optimistic and exhilarated. I think about Sam and imagine him looking down on us, grinning as he watches while we set our plans into action. Every bit of me is trembling with exalted emotion; for a moment I feel so happy and buoyant it's like Sam's not even dead at all. I reach for a mug of tea, relying on the weight of the liquid-filled cup to steady my shaking hands. My heart is pounding and my chest quivers with the vibration. I can't trust my voice so I take a sip of my tea instead, even though the rising steam is a sure sign that this is probably not a good idea. But I don't care. Right now I only care about Sam and the Peace Project.

'We'll draft one standard letter to everyone.' Gloria suddenly speaks again, only this time her speech is more thoughtful and orderly. Her eyes are far away, as if she's consulting an imaginary notepad in the sky. 'But we mustn't forget that not everybody knows about Sam's death.'

Her last word surprises me; its harsh finality seems out of place on her gentle lips. But what else was she expected to say?

'Would you both mind if I wrote this letter on my own?' Gloria's gaze drops from the imaginary notepad down to Mum and me. 'This is for me to do – this is my news to share. I am his mother, after all. I wouldn't want it to come from anyone else.'

Mum and I nod with more oomph than is necessary: *Of course* we understand. *Of course* it's OK.

'I'll write it tonight.' Gloria nods resolutely while she talks. 'And then how about we meet tomorrow morning, at the Peace Project office, around nine?'

Mum and I nod once again.

'Great!' Gloria smiles in a satisfied sort of way and reaches for a ginger biscuit. 'So that's decided then.' She dunks her biscuit in her tea and lifts it quickly to her mouth. She's still caught up in her thoughts but she appears to me to be calmer, more in control. Ten minutes ago her grief was wild and unpredictable. Now it has purpose. Our dedication has provided a channel for the sadness and heartache that was threatening to sink her like the freak wave that swallowed up Sam.

To all our Peace Project friends around the world,

It's been a while since I last made contact with many of you. I've had even fewer dealings with others, as my son Sam has been the point of contact for so much of the United Kingdom's Peace Project correspondence. Our scheduled prayer for peace has been his passion and a fervent mission to which he has dedicated so much of his heart and time. And it's because of Sam that I'm sending this message to you today.

Shortly before Christmas, my beautiful son was killed in an unforeseeable and very tragic accident. The loss of this loving, kind and spirited young man is something that bewilders me. But for those of you who knew my Sam I'm sure you'll agree that - true to style - he'd have hoped for some good to come from this tragedy.

Sam was never reserved about revealing his status as a Bosnian war orphan. And even though he lost his entire birth family as a result of war, he never once wavered from his dream of world peace. Sam was the embodiment of harmony, acceptance and forgiveness. And he lived his life accordingly. It's for this reason that I, along with his best friend Liberty Belle, ask the following of you: to consider dedicating the International Peace Project's prayer for peace to the memory of Samir Pejic, who didn't just believe in our cause - he lived it.

I hope to hear from you.

With best wishes,
Gloria Degabrielle
International Peace Project
UNITED KINGDOM

Mum is reading over my shoulder and reaches the end of Gloria's letter a few moments before me. There are certain parts I have to read twice; my eyes keep retracing their steps back to the term 'Sam's best friend'. The words soothe me, like a hot water bottle pressed up against my belly to ease the cramps that visit every month.

'That's a beautiful letter, Gloria,' Mum says gently.

I'm sitting in front of the computer with my right hand still gripping the mouse. It can't be easy delivering such sad news but Gloria's letter is both touching and strangely uplifting. It's the right sort of letter, the thoughts agree. Lotus, who has been working at the desk behind us, rises from her chair and joins us in front of the computer. She's holding a piece of printed paper.

'This is a list of every country involved in the Peace Project,' she begins. 'You'll find their addresses stored in the email address book. So it's simply a case of pasting the letter into an email, making sure to include every country's address, and sending it off. But it's important that we get this sent out today. After all, we only have four days left until New Year.'

The thoughts are fully charged and optimistic, but even we recognise that this doesn't leave us with very much time at all. There are time differences to consider, as well as the fact that each country has a group of organisers who will have to convene and take a vote on our request. The decision is not simply up to one particular individual. And then of course we mustn't forget that it is the festive season: people are spending time with their families. Some may even be away on holiday. I've been so caught up in the hope and expectation of the idea that I never really stopped to consider the logistics. Can we really do it? What if we run out of days and hours?

But if anyone else is feeling my desperation they're not showing it. Inspired by their optimism, the thoughts resolve to at least give this our very best shot. *Please help us to reach all the Peace Project organisers*, I plead by way of a small, silent prayer. *If You are listening right now, I know I haven't been particularly loyal...but if You are out there, please help us to do this – for Sam.* I think about Shawn and the Spirit she says moves through the natural world and each one of us. That's what we need right now, a loving spirit to guide each one of the Project volunteers stationed around the globe and inspire them to make the right decision.

'I'll send the email out this instant,' I offer. I'm aware of a few mutters of approval from my collaborators but I'm mostly preoccupied with making sure that I include every single country when I add the addresses. I then paste Gloria's letter into the body of the email. I'm about to press Send and launch our plea into cyberspace, but this suddenly seems too blasé. This will be our first and most important email regarding Sam's dedication; it *has* to start us off on a positive note. So I close my eyes and imagine computers sitting in countries all over the world. 'Good luck,' I whisper and then press Send. The email disappears and I'm once again staring at the inbox.

It's almost midday when Lotus enters the cramped Peace Project office. She's carrying a pot of tea and a small round iced cake. 'Come on you two, there's carrot cake and tea,' Lotus calls out to us.

But I remain seated, still facing Mum. 'Have you had any replies yet?' I'm working hard at keeping my voice light and casual and something more than an expectant whisper. I don't want to be the person wondering if we're there yet when we've only just left the driveway, but I can't help myself. I'm not necessarily after a yes or no answer, but an encouraging response of any sort would be very warm and welcoming.

'Nope, nothing yet – sorry,' is Mum's less-than-warm-and-welcoming reply.

It's too soon anyway, the thoughts pipe up. But of course I knew that already.

'Any replies?' Gloria's face is kind and appreciative as she heads into the room.

'What happens if we hear back from every single country except for one or two?' This has been worrying me all morning and it's too much to simply leave to the thoughts to fret over any longer.

Gloria reunites her cup with its saucer and shakes her head, first at the floor and then at eye level. 'Well, I don't really know. I suppose, if that were the case, we could try to get hold of these countries by telephone. Computers do crash, emails do get lost. But my personal feeling is that we've *got* to have every single country on board, in writing or verbally. Otherwise it will seem like a half-hearted farce. And that's worse than no dedication at all.'

Mum and Lotus nod their agreement. And even though I know that Gloria is absolutely right, the idea that we might fail leaves me queasy.

Right now all of Mum's concentration is focused on guiding Aurora in the direction of the Peace Project office. Instead of the placid and soggy soaking rain that is so typical of this country, the sky this morning is dark and angry and lashing out at us with ferocious fingers of icy rain. Aurora's antique wipers are working overtime, sloshing this way and that, trying to keep the windscreen clear and water-free. But today the rain is the stronger competitor and no sooner have the wiper blades cleared an area of glass than it has returned to smudge and smear it all up again.

It's been precisely twenty-three hours and twelve minutes since we sent the email. I'm surprised by my nervousness; the thoughts are taking over my head. *What if NOBODY has replied? That's silly – people care, they'll reply. That's if they get the email in time. But of course they'll be checking their mail! There are, after all, only three days left before our scheduled prayer for peace – there are still things left to organise (surely they'll realise this?). Yes, that makes sense, but we still don't know for cert—*

'Mum, what do you expect we'll find when we check the Peace Project inbox?' My head is beginning to ache; I have to say something out loud to override the thoughts.

'Uh, not now Libby darling, please. I must concentrate on the road. I've never seen so much rain!'

I don't want to end up in a ditch (especially not without checking for emails first), so I remain quiet for the remainder of the journey and stare through the window. When we finally arrive at the Peace Project office I'm the first to notice Gloria's car outside the entrance. Mum's too busy parking by ear.

'Oh, for the sake of Gaia!' she cries out only moments after Aurora's rear fender makes contact with the brick wall of the Project building. The crunch is audible over the sound of rain slapping against the car's old metal.

I already have my door open; the rain on my left hand is cold and sharp. 'Come on Mum, we'll worry about that later.' It's not like Aurora will even notice one more battle scar.

Thankfully Mum doesn't argue and opens her door to leap out into the rain. We leg it for the entrance and quickly disappear inside the warm dry sanctity of the Peace Project office. Lotus is busy dividing the contents of a thermos flask between four mugs while Gloria is sitting in front of a computer. Both women glance up as we enter.

'So how many replies have we received then?' I suppose I should have said good morning first.

Gloria smiles her greeting and I instantly recognise it as the kind you wear on your face when you're not sure what else to do with it – the motion without the emotion. It's not a good sign.

'So far only three, I'm afraid,' she responds. 'And only two of these were positive replies, although Samoa promises to get back to us shortly.' Gloria rises from her chair and heads for a steaming mug.

'Well, it was nice of them to acknowledge our email in the meantime,' Mum comments in her usual the-glass-is-half-full fashion.

'Yeh, whatever,' I mutter and head for the other computer which is still lifeless and sleeping. I boot it up and wait patiently for all the start-up blah blah to slide past the screen. The desktop finally appears and I click-to-open the bottom-right stud of the Outlook icon and head straight for the inbox. And it's just as Gloria said: we have two definite yes votes. Yemen and Chad would be more than happy to dedicate their leg of the prayer for peace to Sam's memory. They've sent their heartfelt condolences too. Yemen, especially, believes that a young man like Sam will be genuinely missed. They had exchanged regular correspondence with my best friend for some time, it seems.

I'm vaguely aware of someone claiming the empty computer beside me but I'm completely caught up in the issue of our largely unanswered email plea and so I don't take much notice of who or why. Instead I press the Send/Receive button and wait for the inbox to refresh. There are still no further replies.

'This keyboard is broken.'

The voice is louder in my right ear. I turn towards the sound, which is coming from the direction of the other computer. Lotus is sitting in the chair in front of the computer Gloria recently abandoned.

'What are you doing, Lotus?' I ask.

'I'm going to email all the countries again and gently remind them that we are working to a very tight deadline.'

The idea's not half bad. 'But I thought you weren't very good with computers?'

'I'm not, but there's only one way to learn.' She has both hands poised over the keyboard and is flexing her fingers twinkle-little-star style. 'Except I'll need a keyboard that works,' she adds firmly.

'What makes you think that one is broken?'

'Our password is "serenity", right?' I nod. 'Well, no matter what I type all I get are little stars.'

If I weren't so concerned I think I might have burst a blood vessel laughing. But I'm staring blankly instead. 'It's supposed to do that, Lotus.'

'Well, how does the computer know if I'm using the correct password if it only keys in stars?'

I glance over my shoulder. I think I may need Mum or Gloria's help here – something tells me that Lotus is not going to give up easily. But both women are bent over and studying something on paper with their backs to me. I'm stuck with this one.

'Lotus, the computer shows the asterisks so that no one else looking on can see your password. It's for security. The keyboard and computer are working fine.'

Lotus pulls a face like she just smelled dog poo but thankfully doesn't add anything further. Relieved, I return to my own computer and the thoughts. But the peaceful silence doesn't last much longer than thirty seconds.

'Now I'm carefully typing the word serenity into the password box but the computer keeps telling me it's incorrect. When I know it's not! Stupid asterisks. Stupid computer.'

I stare at Lotus for a few moments and then quietly

get up from my chair and stand beside her.

'See!' She demonstrates the process by retyping the word serenity, forcefully jabbing the keys with pointed fingers. It's then that I notice the small green light of the Caps Lock, indicating the function is on.

Ah, right. 'You need to type the password in lower case,' I explain patiently. It's a small mistake, anybody could make it.

Lotus laughs and rolls her eyes. 'And I thought I was the novice.' She tut-tuts while she gestures to the keyboard and the neat square keys topped with printed letters. 'Isn't it obvious – this is a capital letter keyboard.'

For a moment or two I'm at a loss. But then I realise that the woman is being serious. And what this means is that I'm now going to have to teach her all about the Caps Lock and upper and lower case and *ooh crickey*! I take a deep breath and begin the lesson. Lotus has the sense to listen and when I'm done, seems to accept that the keyboard is working just fine and able to create big and small letters. By the time I return to my own computer the minute hand of the clock on the wall has moved ten times. I realise then that it will take Lotus forever to open up a new blank email, let alone compose any sort of gentle reminder to send out to the

Peace Project countries. But she seems so determined. And it is a good idea. Perhaps I should compose an email too; Lotus and the others might just approve. I would keep it short and polite and definitely avoid sounding pushy. It might just work. I'm about to get started when—

'Liberty?'

She's back. I can just see her out of the corner of my right eye; she's studying the keyboard very closely. 'Yes, Lotus?' There's a small silent pause.

'Where's the smiley key?'

Exasperation takes my face and pinches it into a frown. But I don't have time to protest because my computer suddenly pings with a new email message. And there in the inbox, displayed in bold, is an unread email from Peace Project Malta. This is exactly what I've been waiting for, but I'm suddenly extremely nervous of opening it. What happens if one country – just *one single country*, refuses our request? Gloria said that it would be pointless if every country didn't give us their yes vote.

'Don't you know either?' Lotus is staring at me expectantly. She's still thinking about smilies.

'We have another reply – from Malta!' I announce to the room. Suddenly I'm surrounded by three eager women.

'Go on, open it,' Mum urges me on.

And so I do.

Dear Gloria,

Please accept our sincere condolences. Sam was special young man who will never be forgotten and we at Peace Project Malta will be honoured to dedicate our prayer for peace to his memory.

With our very best wishes,
Carmelo Assopardi and Peace Project Malta team

Suddenly there's another ping – another new email message! This one is from Peace Project Vietnam.

'Wonderful,' Gloria coos. 'Quickly, open it.'

This time I don't even stop to consider my nerves and hastily click-to-open. My first read through is nothing more than a speedy skimming of the message. My eyes snag on keywords like 'warm sympathy' and 'deepest wishes'. And then there they are – the words I've been searching for: 'Without reserve we offer our prayer for peace to the memory of Sam'.

'That's four down and another 188 to go,' Mum says brightly. There's silence as her face dims with a small look of regret. 'Well, we are making progress,' she adds quickly.

Yes, we're certainly making progress, the thoughts agree. But at this rate will we ever hear back from everyone in time?

Mick stopped by the cottage yesterday morning with the news that we'd received a whopping seventy-eight email replies. And every single country said *yes!* (Those who knew Sam said they felt privileged to deliver their prayer for peace with his memory held fast in their hearts and their minds.)

This was the first time I'd seen Mick for a while, but I didn't give much thought to how I felt about seeing my mum's Sixties-hippy, sandal-loving boyfriend again. After all that's happened, perhaps I really don't care very much anymore. There are more important things for the thoughts to worry about. But I did feel slightly resentful that he'd visited the Peace Project offices. I may not have set eyes on Mick for a while but I know he's been around, in the background, helping out here and there, so it wasn't his interference that surprised or bothered me. But thanks to Mick the enthusiastic messenger, yesterday I no longer had any reason to head off to the Peace Project office. And without the Project to occupy my time, the day ahead lay spread out before me like a vast muddy river. And it passed just as slowly.

The rain that's been pelting our roof tiles and heads since practically Christmas has finally dried up. Right now I'm lying in Mum's bed listening to the quiet. The radio alarm clock on the bedside table is flashing 7:23 in red square numbers. We're leaving for the office at 8:30. I have time. Gloria called last night to say that another twenty-three emails had filtered through and I'm curled up in bed doing the maths. That's another eighty-seven yes replies we're still waiting on. And we have approximately forty hours and thirty-seven minutes left until midnight on the 31st of December. The clock is now flashing 7:24. Make that forty hours and thirty-six minutes. I think my second task of the morning – the one after I've checked the Project's inbox – is to compose an email firmly updating the remaining countries on my calculations. Lotus's draft is still not quite completed. But I'll have to make sure I don't email those countries that have already responded…don't want to harass anyone…might be time-consuming…but then I have time…a whole day…mmm. Flash 7:25 flash. I'm so busy with the thoughts I don't even hear Mum entering the bedroom.

Vegetarians Die Healthier. Well that's what it says on

the pyjama top in front of me. Mum is staring down at my sprawled shape. Her short white hair is hidden by a colourful striped beanie hat and she's holding a brown-wrapped parcel. She holds it out to me.

'For you.'

'Me?'

'Post came.'

'Who from?'

'Not sure.'

'Oh.'

'Mmm.'

We both stare blankly at the parcel for a few moments; neither of us are morning people. I slowly rotate the package and examine it from every angle. There's only my address and a couple of stamps on its surface, nothing more. I should probably just open it.

'Why don't you just open it,' Mum suggests.

Inside the brown wrapping is a small velvety bag tied at the neck with a soft pale yellow ribbon. There's also a letter. I open this first.

Dear Libby,

This bracelet is made from chrysocolla beads - a traditional Native American healing stone associated with tranquillity and peace, patience and unconditional love. Wear it when you say your prayer for peace, and any time you feel lost or alone. I hope it will remind you of our friendship, and lead you to a place of inner balance, peace and understanding. Sometimes all we need is something to remind us to keep on trying.

Until we meet again,
Shawn Two-Rivers Redd

I wordlessly pass the letter over to Mum, who is still hovering over me, and then focus my attention on the bag with the ribbon. The small bow unravels easily and I shake the bag's contents into my waiting palm. Chrysocolla beads, I discover, are an extraordinary blend of aqua and teal colours that gleam and shimmer like the oily pattern on a peacock's feathers. The stones are lightweight, smooth and round in my hand – each one like a miniature earth as seen from outer space. There's a slip of paper inside the bag too. I unfold it carefully – again, Shawn's handwriting.

Hold on to what is good,
Even if it's a handful of earth.
Hold on to what you believe,
Even if it's a tree that stands by itself.
Hold on to what you must do,
Even if it's a long way from here.
Hold on to your life,
Even if it's easier to let go.
Hold on to my hand,
Even if someday I'll be gone away from you.
A PUEBLO INDIAN PRAYER

I know the prayer was sent to me by Shawn, and yet it makes me think about Sam. Perhaps that's what Shawn Two-Rivers Redd intended all along. The thought stretches my face with a very small smile.

And that smile remains attached to my face for almost the entire journey to the Peace Project office. It's only when the drab brick building comes into full view that I once again begin to fret over the Project inbox, wondering whether it's empty or full of replies that have the word *no* pinned to their tails. But then again (if I think it through properly), it's unlikely that any country would simply say 'no'. They'd probably be more diplomatic and reply with phrases like 'of course we'd like to, but we really don't think…' or 'unfortunately the vote was not unanimous…' There I go again, afraid of what *might* be. My fingers find their way to the blue-green beads wrapped around my wrist. 'Hold on to what you must do,' I recite in a whisper. If Mum hears my prayer she doesn't say anything.

We're the first ones in the office and I head straight for a computer while Mum fiddles with some papers before pulling up a chair beside me. And together we wait and watch as the inbox fills with incoming emails, both silently counting each one with a tiny dip of our heads. When the messages finally do stop coming, the total tally in bold brackets stands at fifty-one brand-new, unread emails.

Mum is the first to speak. 'That's great!' She touches my shoulder.

'It is if they say yes,' I reply with a confident rattle of my beads.

Mum reaches for the original printed list of Peace Project countries and a pencil. 'You read the mails and I'll mark them off.'

It's an efficient system and after half an hour or so we have our final score. That's fifty-one 'absolutely/it would be an honour/without a doubt' replies! I grin up at

Mum, who also looks delighted with the result.

'Only thirty-six more to go,' she says with visible relief, 'and it's still not quite ten o'clock.'

'I think we're going to do it.' I'm still smiling, only now it's at the computer screen. 'I really think we're going to do it.'

twenty-six
taking kicks

'Samoa said no.'

'What do you mean Samoa said no?' Mum cries out. The news sucks the strength from her so that she only just manages to hang on to the shopping bags she's toting.

'They finally came back to us. And they said no.' Gloria shrugs sadly. Her face is a blink away from tears. 'Apparently they've thought long and hard about it and while of course they send their heartfelt condolences, they feel that Sam's dedication doesn't relate to the overall Peace Project mission statement.' She shrugs once again, like it's something for her to do… something, *anything*.

'But do they know *all* about Sam's past…about Bosnia?' I finally manage to speak.

Another shrug. Gloria appears lost.

Suddenly I'm babbling. 'But our prayer for peace carries the message of love and harmony. Our aim is for people to live and act in the spirit of its message – to be compassionate, respectful and accepting of one another.

And Sam represented all of these things – he believed in these values, regardless of all that he'd seen and been through…and the family he'd lost. Perhaps they just need some convincing. Gloria, you must phone Samoa.' I'm facing her with laser-beam eyes and a determined jaw.

'I've thought about that.' But she doesn't sound convinced.

'We can't give up this easily, not now! You have to phone them. They need to understand.'

This time Gloria finally nods. 'I will phone,' she says, 'but I'd like to be alone when I do so.'

There's just Mum and me here and we both quickly nod and instinctively take one step backwards. 'We'll be back in a short while,' Mum smiles reassuringly and shuffles out of the office still clutching her shopping bags. I follow and close the door behind us. We pause for a moment, both silent and staring at each other with faces of fear. With only one day and thirty-six countries to go, could this all still go horribly wrong?

Aurora takes us to Le French Café with its dangling fake flowers. I look around for the waitress – I haven't forgotten her refusal to display my Missing poster – but today she seems to have been replaced by another waitress, who is fake-tanned to a shiny fluorescent orange. Still, she appears much happier to serve us than the other waitress was. She's even willing to make light chit-chat while Mum and I break blueberry muffins into small pieces and shove them around our plates with our full and silent attention focussed on our luminous waitress. Apparently this job at Le French Café is just a way for her to earn extra money. She's really a figure skater. Semi-professional. Soon. Hopefully. And it's thanks to her chatter about split flips, triple toe loops and camel spins that a full hour passes before Mum and I return to Aurora and the Peace Project office.

The room is empty. Gloria is nowhere to be found. This doesn't look good. With nothing else to do and the thoughts to occupy, I sit myself down in front of the computer to check emails. Again. We have twenty-three new email messages. I open and scroll through each one. They're all yes votes. I'm not elated. In fact I've barely even made it to interested. What's the point if Samoa says no?

Suddenly the door opens and Gloria enters, followed by Lotus. They're both smiling. Now Gloria is giving us the thumbs-up. 'I told Samoa a little more about Sam. They understand and they're on board.'

Now I'm interested. 'Woohoo!' I cheer.

'That makes it thirteen more to go,' Mum sums up merrily.

There's a brief moment of *now-what?* silence before Gloria speaks again. 'A watched pot never boils, ladies. And there's something I have wanted to do for some time now.' Nobody interrupts to ask the obvious, we all patiently wait for Gloria to set her own pace. She swallows and breathes deep before continuing.

'I want to commemorate Sam's final moments alive. I want to leave flowers near the groyne…the one you and Sam walked along, Libby.'

The sudden mention of my name almost frightens me. And the thought of returning to the groyne terrifies me even more. I suddenly feel implicated; once again I feel the squeeze of guilt. But Gloria's face is open and kind – she wants me to share in the moment and acknowledge Sam's life alongside her. And then I'm suddenly grateful that she thought to include me. I gulp and nod and Mum grips my hand as we all make our way outside to Aurora and the groyne I never anticipated ever seeing again.

We buy flowers along the way and head down to the beach where I am strangely surprised to discover that everything is exactly as it was when I was last here with Sam. Nothing has changed with his passing. The noticeboard printed with pictures encased in faded yellow triangles is still there. And the sign that warns 'Caution – This Beach Is Not Lifeguarded' has not changed either. It all feels a bit surreal – being here again, only this time with Mum, Gloria and Lotus. But it isn't quite as scary as I had expected. In a strange way, I can almost feel Sam's warmth beside me again. And as we make our way down to the water's edge I find myself scanning the waves that once held Sam and me fast. Perhaps a part of me is still searching for some understanding, or maybe in my heart I'm still looking for him.

But Gloria won't let this moment turn as grey as the skies. She grips her flowers and quickly throws them hard and far out into the chaotic waves, shouting out her love for Sam as she does so. Then it's Lotus, and then Mum, and then my turn. 'I love you, Sam!' I shout out the very moment the bunch of white daisies leaves my hand to soar high into the sea air. My words are gone with the wind before the flowers have even touched water, but I feel like they will remain here for ever, echoing against the sea cliffs.

We watch our flowers float out, heading for the horizon, and then walk along the beach, hand in hand. We walk all the way to the very end and back again. By the time we return to Aurora we're almost frozen on the outside, and yet inside I feel warm. I feel a sense of hope that everything might just be OK again.

Back at the Peace Project office we're all comfortably silent while we clutch mugs of hot tea and defrost. I'm thinking about Sam's daisies and wondering where they've floated off to, but I'm also thinking about the Peace Project inbox. Will our remaining thirteen yes votes be in yet? I'm almost too nervous to look. But I don't have to, because Lotus is first at the computer.

'We have thirteen replies!' she announces excitedly. She waits for us to huddle around her before opening each one up. Today there is an extra-special bond between us, we're all in complete sync with one another and without any urging or prompting, begin to read each new message out in unison. Together we count down our collection of yes votes until we have just one more to go. This final message is from South Africa. We just need one more yes.

'This one's for you, Libby,' Gloria says as she turns to face with me with a gentle smile. 'This was all your idea. You read this one out loud.'

The thoughts, for once, are calm. There's no doubt we're nervous, but not knowing is even worse. The time has well and truly come. So Lotus clicks to open and

I begin reading with a clear voice.

'Dear Gloria, we are touched by your offer to play a part in your son Sam's dedication and will be honoured to hold his memory in our hearts as we say our prayer for world peace. You are both in our thoughts. With love and light from South Africa.'

We did it. We really and truly did it.

Where I'm standing feels especially cold. With nothing to create shelter or offer protection, every one of us is exposed to the full spite of the bitter Atlantic breeze. But at least it's not raining. That's what I keep reminding myself as I stretch my thick coat tighter around me and bury my head deeper into its upturned collar. The brilliant light of the moon above is proving useful too. I don't think I've ever seen it quite so bright before. The satellite is quite literally a glowing ball of white, casting luminous moonbeams and illuminating our surroundings and each other like a powerful floodlight.

With only twenty minutes still remaining the gathering on the cliff top is impressive. Gloria chose this spot. And not one of the Peace Project United Kingdom members objected. The Christian Orthodox Church is a dark solemn shape that watches over us quietly – significant only as the place some of us came to say goodbye to Sam. His funeral seems to belong to another lifetime.

I'm just looking around, not saying much, a pair of eyes blinking over a corduroy collar. Most of these people have travelled hours to get here, many by train, some even by plane. I only know this because they're telling each other *you'll-never-believe-this-but* stories involving tickets, terminals and knuckle-gnawing delays. Few have actually met before, but that doesn't matter. They're all happily putting faces to the email addresses on the Peace Project United Kingdom mailing list.

It's almost five o'clock on the very first morning of the New Year. The day of the international prayer for peace has finally come. There are 193 countries and we'll each take our turn to say a prayer – one every seven minutes. By the end of the first day of this brand new year every single country will have said a prayer. Many countries, starting with Iceland just after midnight, will already have said theirs. This is something to keep thinking about. It is, after all, a universal effort (a little fact Mum, Lotus and Gloria – our official Peace Project organisers – keep mentioning as gentle reminders while they meet and greet their partners in peace).

Not far away, just to my left, Mick and a short man wearing a deerstalker hat and drainpipe trousers are busy filling cups with tea and coffee poured from large silver urns that glint in the moon's light. Everybody appears quite at ease, as if meeting before dawn at the edge of this cliff top is something we all do quite regularly. I'm pacing to keep warm and soothe my nerves. Gloria's nervous too, I can tell by the way she's speaking loudly and pumping each word and facial expression brimful of energy. We're number forty-one in the queue; our prayer begins at 5.10 am sharp.

Something's finally starting to happen. Bodies are shuffling, cups are being drained or abandoned and the even hum of general conversation has peaked in frequency. People suddenly seem excited. I edge closer. Gloria and Lotus are gently corralling the peace lovers into formation – we're moving towards a circle shape. Now we're linking hands. A woman in a cape jacket and tight pants claims my left hand so I shove the right one in my pocket. I'm searching for Mum; I really want her to stand beside me. There she is, surveying the crowd. My neighbour's hand feels dry and strange in my own, which isn't very peace-and-love of me so I try to appear casual but my fingers are awkward and twitching. Finally Mum's walking in my direction. I notice that Mick is in tow. I'm still thinking peace-and-love thoughts so I don't let that bother me. But I want Mum holding my hand so I keep it hidden until she's close by.

Gloria has also joined the human chain – she's a few links down to our right. And one by one people are slowly falling silent. Those who still seem to find things to say finally hush when Gloria begins clearing her throat. My guess is that she's imagined this moment many times over already.

'It's wonderful that we could all come together. Thank you to each and every one of you for making the journey,' she begins. Her eyes are bright and shiny, reflecting the moon's light and slowly rolling this way and that as she gently makes contact with the gaze of those around her.

'We all know why we're here and what we hope to achieve by the joining together of our hands and hearts. It is our shared values and principles that have brought us here today. But before we begin I'd like to ask you all to please close your eyes for a moment. With your support, I'd like to take a moment and dedicate this prayer for peace to the memory of Sam – a beautiful soul and my darling son. He was a young man who lived his short life with such love and compassion. He left this world a much better place and will never be forgotten. Bless you, Sam, this is *your* dream.'

Everyone is silent. I can feel my chest constricting with the pressure of the emotion surging through me.

Yes, bless you, Sam, the thoughts echo. I lift my gaze to the moon glowing like a halo above our heads. Its round perfect shape is changing; the moon is slowly disappearing behind the dark bulk of a thick, shifting cloud. I'm mesmerised by the sight of the shrinking moon. And then it's suddenly gone. Now there's only black sky.

And then the inkiness begins to twinkle. I blink my eyes and refocus; perhaps I've been staring too long. But when I open my eyes it's still there – a spectacular panorama of bottomless black sky pitted with the sharp shiny twinkles of glittering stars. The view is breathtaking. Heaven has turned on its lights. Yes, I see you, Sam.

They say that when it's dark enough you can see the stars. I believed I had lost everything – my family, my soul mate and myself. And yet somehow, through it all, I discovered that my world has simply changed, not ended. There is now a different me. Like the light from those stars travelling to earth, perhaps we're all on our personal journeys. Well, that's what the thoughts think anyway.

The End

Other Orchard books you might enjoy

Orchard books are available from all good bookshops, or can be ordered direct from the publisher: Orchard Books, PO BOX 29, Douglas IM99 1BQ
Credit card orders please telephone 01624 836000
or fax 01624 837033 or visit our website: www.orchardbooks.co.uk
or email: bookshop@enterprise.net for details.

To order please quote title, author and ISBN
and your full name and address.
Cheques and postal orders should be made payable to 'Bookpost plc.'
Postage and packing is FREE within the UK
(overseas customers should add £1.00 per book).

Prices and availability are subject to change.